EVERDARK

JT LAWRENCE
COLBY R. RICE

FIRE FINCH

1

SMOKE, STARS, AND SHATTERED DREAMS

ALATHIA

We collapsed on the bed, out of breath and sweating. The hot sheets tangled us together as if we were one glowing, panting creature. Warm skin and damp cotton. I closed my eyes, enjoying the lingering pleasure that leaped like amber flames throughout my body. If my heart were alive, it would have been racing in its cage. I lifted a hand to my damp forehead and pushed away the long dark hair that clung to it, and finally opened my eyes.

The human, propped up on his elbow, gazed at me, chin in hand. He had good hands. A great body. Good lips, too, and pale blue crystalline eyes that always seemed to want to devour me. My eyes were drawn to his neck. Little did he know that if anyone were to do the devouring, it would be me.

"Stop staring," I said.

The smell of the city air filled my penthouse apartment: smoke, stars, and shattered dreams. His expression became less earnest, the smoldering replaced by a hint of a smile.

"I can't help it," he said. "You're just so goddamn beautiful."

The lights flickered as if they were afraid of what he would say next; a warning to keep his mouth shut.

Oh shit, I thought. *He's going to say it.*

"Don't say it," I wanted to tell him. "Don't ruin the perfect thing we've got going. Fantastic hook-ups, uncomplicated by the pulsing thunderclouds of emotion that threaten other relationships. We agreed, no strings attached, remember? We agreed: no dates, no professions of affection, no tangled feelings."

I pulled the sheet away from my body so that it no longer connected us. I needed space; needed to breathe.

Up until then, tenderness and deep physical satisfaction marked Frank's and my meetings. It had been going so well. But humans are funny that way. They don't know when they've got a good thing going. They always want more. Extra, further, higher, deeper. They don't realize that their constant striving will be the end of them. Annoyed and overheated, I pushed the sheets even further away.

My naked body, pale as death, made Frank's smile disappear, and his face light up. A fire behind a screen.

"I—" he began.

"Don't say it," I urged him.

I moved to climb out of my luxurious king-sized bed. Frank grabbed my wrist and I turned to look at him. His eyes were wide and wanting.

"Alathia," he said.

His strong grip froze both of us in place. I surrendered. A shame, but I surrendered. I looked deep into his eyes and our souls touched.

"I have to stop seeing you," he said.

I didn't break eye contact. "Yes."

He looked confused, as if he didn't know where his words had come from. He let go of my wrist. "It's over."

"Yes," I said again. "I understand."

He was frowning at me as I stood and made my way to my porcelain-tiled bathroom. He watched me as I moved, my body slim and impossibly white-skinned. My fangs sharp against my tongue, I didn't turn to see his expression as I turned on the water and the steam rose within the large glass cubicle.

"Lock the door on your way out."

Sleep proved impossible after the human left, and I lay on the scented sheets, tossing and turning. Sleep doesn't come easy to me at the best of times, but I was feeling especially restless. I'd miss Frank. Or, rather, I'd miss the sex. He was always willing, and easy, and he was a generous lover. I sighed at the ceiling. I wasn't pleased at the inconvenience. I'd have to find someone new.

Just as I felt myself drifting off, my phone chirped. I grabbed it from my bedside table. The app told me the security alarm at the office had been set off. I swore loudly in Croatian, then sat up and tapped the screen to check the camera footage. It had been wiped. I cursed again and dropped the phone. A shot of adrenaline launched me out of bed, and I pulled on a black jumpsuit and matching jacket. Silver-toed leather boots. Silk infinity scarf. Antique revolver.

I raced out of my apartment and flew down the stairs like a motion blur. I can move quickly, faster than any elevator. Especially my building's elevator, which is a huge gold contraption, built more for looks than speed. It plays classical music. Enough said.

The streets were wet and black, and the dark puddles of rain shimmered with oily rainbows. My driver flashed his lights at me, and as I neared the sleek Jaguar, the back door opened automatically. I climbed in and slammed it shut.

"Good evening, Miss Laurent," Edgar said, turning to face me. "Where will I be taking you this evening?"

"There's been a break-in," I said. "At the office."

Edgar knew me well enough to not ask for details or offer to call the police. Perhaps because he was British, he never mentioned my strange working hours, my rather considerable assortment of lovers, or the fact that I never seem to grow old. He used to be my age—younger, even—when he began working for me. Now his body is slowly collapsing inward, and his skin has become a map of the places he's been, the things he's seen. I'd guess he was around eighty years old, but he didn't drive like it.

As he put his foot down, the G-force pushed me back into my charcoal suede seat. Within fifteen minutes, we were out of the suburbs and in the middle of the bustling city. There was no time to park. Edgar pulled to the side of the road, his orange hazard lights flashing, and he pushed the button on the dashboard that levered my door open for me. He was a gentleman like that.

"Thanks, Edgar," I said. "This shouldn't take long."

The access pad at the entrance to the building had been fried. Wires stuck out of the usually neat interface and the biometric screen was smashed. It was all for show.

The company I use—BlackJack Security—is the best you can get in Johannesburg. The first rung access pad is indestructible, despite its appearance. Someone wanted me to think they had breached the system by destroying the pad with a small, targeted charge, but I knew better. Brute force is no way to break into this particular building. Did they want me to think it was a coincidence? That someone passing by decided to try their luck and didn't know they were breaking into the offices of Laurent & Shaw Private Investigators, the most talented detective duo in the city? Not the smartest move, especially as we were one part vampire, one part werewolf.

No, this was no coincidence. Whoever did this had a stealth hacker on board, and I knew from personal experience that they don't come cheap. I swung open the heavy glass doors and launched up the stairs. The access pad on the wall outside our office was in a state similar to the one on the street, burnt and shattered, and now I smelled the electrical smoke in the air. With a silent breath, I reached for my gun, clicked off the safety and held it out in front of me. I nudged open the broken doors slowly, quietly, and stepped inside.

Despite the dark, but I knew what awaited me because the smell changed from ozone sparks to fresh blood. My nose twitched. I hadn't eaten all day, which always heightened my sense of smell, especially where the red stuff is concerned. On a hungry day, I can smell blood spatter from a mile off. But judging by how my saliva was streaming into my mouth, this was more than a splash against a wall. I found myself wishing I had Sami's lupine night vision. Mine is good, but hers is on fleek. My fingers tightened around the carved ivory handle of my revolver as I crept farther inside. Finger pressed up against the trigger, my breath came in shallow waves. The reception area was empty, the security cameras destroyed. I followed the scent of red copper into the twin office Samira and I shared. Slowly and methodically, I checked for the intruder, but it soon became clear that I was the only one in the room breathing. Revolver in one hand, I reached out with the other for the wall and flicked on the lights. Flinching at what I saw, my stomach lurched. Lowering my trembling gun, I drew back, blinking the nightmarish vision away, but the more I looked, the more vivid it became.

2

BABY BURGERS

SAMIRA

THE WOLF in me didn't like kids. Not alive, at least.

Behind my gaze, the wolf's eyes followed the short fleshy bodies across the plain. Across the grass. I meant grass. We got things confused like that. Parks became "hunting grounds." Groups became "packs." People became "food." Didn't matter what it was, her knowledge of the world as wolf always intruded on mine as human. Especially because she thought her worldview was better.

Can't lie. It was. Most of the time, anyway. Right now, though? I needed her to take several seats. We had a job to do.

I could feel her phantom wolf's tongue flick around my chops. My ears pricked up, and at the same time her internal canine whine squeaked from my throat; she was annoyed by my inferior aural acuity. Still, she listened to the shrieks of joy and glee—and adrenaline coursed through my veins as she mistook the puerile shrieks for the sounds of injured prey. *Vulnerable* prey.

"I think you need to calm down," I muttered. I forced a smile as I handed out another flyer to a passerby. "This is Central Park. Not a hunting ground."

Not a hunting ground ... not yet.

Her responding whimper wound around my head, and I knew that it was just a matter of time before she took over again. Not that I could blame her. The full moon was just three days away, and the more that time ticked down, the more restless she got. Even as the runt of the litter, we'd always had a hard time controlling what came so naturally to us: the urge to roam, the urge to hunt.

The urge to kill.

It was an instinct that was centuries old, bred into countless generations of werewolf and burgeoned by our immortality. And no matter what the higher-ups said was best for our race, werewolves could not suppress our instincts. They might as well tell us not to breathe.

Smiling, laughter, and lip gloss, were the only ways I ever got through it. So I put on my extra-wide cheesy smile as I paced—er, *walked*, and I waved the flyers in my hand.

"Come on, folks! Step right up, step right up! Throw your hat into the ring for a shot at two FREE cruise tickets to—"

Baby burgers.

"BABY BURGERS!"

One couple stopped short and gaped at me, both their eyes wide. The man in the pair creased his brow. "Wait, what?"

"I MEAN, THE *BAHAMAS*!!" I nearly screeched, and I scratched my head as my face flushed. "TOTALLY meant the Bahamas!" I chuckled nervously, and still staring at me, the couple hurried down the street.

I groaned. "Thanks a lot, Wolf Sami. That was a real winner."

Anytime.

"Bitch ..."

She grinned, but I didn't have any more time to wag my finger at her. Really, I had to get more people to opt-in for this raffle or the Happy Days Orphanage was going to shut down for good. The werewolf within didn't seem to care, but I did. It was bad enough that I'd grown up alone. There was no way I was going to let that happen to these kids too.

The alluring jingle of the Mr. Softee ice cream truck danced into my ears, and when I looked up, I saw it bopping its way down the block.

The Happy Days kids in the park were already shouting and running over, swarming me. I was assaulted with hugs, tugs, and desperate shouts for different flavors.

"All right, all right, you little savages!" I chuckled. "Line up and order. And get only one each."

They did, and by the time I'd grabbed my wallet and made it back to the truck, the ice cream guy was already done handing out the cones. He grinned at me as though someone was yanking his dick. "That'll be $369.36."

Yeesh.

I nearly died inside as I gave him the money, *my* hard-earned, blood-sweat-and-plenty-o'-tears money. My jaw dropped as he then handed me ten extra ice creams. The little heathens.

So there I stood, barely holding on to all these extra cones. As I walked back to my booth, I wondered if I should try to throw in a free ice cream cone with each raffle ticket sale—and then I saw him.

A stranger.

Tall and broad, sun-kissed skin, dark eyes. He stood in the middle of the group of kids—my kids—showing them a magic trick.

On instinct, the wolf's hackles rose. The last thing I needed was some weird pedo sniffing around. Still, I walked forward with a smile, just in case I was wrong. And if I was right?

Well ... the wolf in me was hungry.

3

LUCKILY, VAMPIRES DON'T PANIC

ALATHIA

OH, my God.

I swallowed my scream. My mouth was dry.

I was all for *avant-garde* interior design, but this was too much. I blinked again, tried to stay calm, tried to separate the reality from the hallucination. Because this had to be an hallucination, right? There was no way this could be real. Luckily, vampires don't panic.

Pinned to the wall opposite me—the wall previously covered in tasteful cream pinstripe wallpaper—was a dead man in a sharp business suit. My mind raced. I didn't recognize him. Why was he here?

He had a strong body and an average face. Probably close to good-looking on a good day, when things were going his way and his heart was beating. I could tell he'd had good days because his suit was expensive and well-tailored. Too bad blood coated his platinum cufflinks.

I swallowed again and took a step forward, then another, wanting to inspect the corpse. The intense odor of blood was emanating from his stigmata, where industrial size nails penetrated his flesh and fastened him to the wall. Blood had cascaded from each wound, staining the wallpaper and puddling on the carpet below. He had stopped bleeding recently. His body was already cold.

I didn't know the guy, but my hands and feet twinged in empathy. It must have been a horrible way to die. My nerves were buzzing under my skin and in my ears, a kind of static anxiety. Only a sadistic psychopath would do this to a human. Which meant that there was a psycho out there who had a problem with Sami or me, knew where we worked, and had no problem with murder by torture. He or she also knew how to hack our security system.

Something different from the nails that pinned the rest of his body affixed the dead man's right hand. I moved closer, trying to see what the object was. The stink of his vital fluids made my bile rise. Congealed blood always makes me feel ill. I'm not like some of those neophyte vamps who'll try any blood product in any form. I have standards. Mine has to be completely fresh, on tap, warm. Or at least, it used to be, in the Halcyon days. Now it's frowned upon to feed on the real stuff. They tell us it's not safe, that human blood is full of toxins and heavy metals and pathogens, but honestly, when has a vampire ever worried about disease? We're immune to disease. We're immune to death ... mostly.

The main reason we refrain from bleeding the humans now is because they came too close to discovering we were real. Too many vampires, too greedy, too careless. There were witness reports. Medical files with damning evidence. A documentary on Netflix that uncovered way too much. We had to retreat and find another way, or the Masquerade would fall, and our kin would be found out and extinguished. You should never get on the wrong side of a crowd of sheeple with pitchforks, especially if they're scared. Scared humans are unpredictable; dangerous. We had to find another way to live or risk collapsing the Masquerade, and if that happened, no one would be safe. Humans, vampires, werewolves ... I didn't want to be around for that civil war.

I pulled on a latex glove from my desk drawer and yanked the object out of his right hand. His arm fell to his side, leaving a gaping black hole in the wall. The offending thing was a pair of unusual-looking scissors. It looked like a collector's item; a relic from bygone days. Long and thin and straight, like silver daggers joined by a bolt. An intricate pattern was etched into the small handles, with something carved into the blade—words—undecipherable through the crimson paint that covered it. I'd have to check it for fingerprints and clean it up. But first I had to call someone.

Samira Shaw's phone rang five times before she picked up.

"Hey, Alla," she said. She sounded distracted. Her mouth was too close to the receiver as if she had the phone wedged in between her cheek and her shoulder. It was noisy in the background. People talking, kids laughing. I could practically feel the sun streaming through the phone. I'm not a fan of sunshine.

I looked out of our huge office window and saw the city lights twinkling like stars you don't yet know are dead.

It was dark, quiet.

"Sami," I said. "Who did you piss off this time?"

4

MAYBE THAT WAS A LITTLE FORWARD

SAMIRA

CUTE GUY. Sniff his ass. Or eat him, whatever.

"Can you *please*?"

I bit my words back with a smile, and as I walked up to the new john, I forced the wolf into my mental cage.

The guy was already smiling at me as I closed the distance.

"Hello, kind sir!" I put on my best game face. "Are you interested in buying raffle tickets for a trip to the Bahamas? It's for a good cause. We're raising money for the orphanage."

SPLAT! A cold glob slapped onto my toes and melted down in between them, ruining my sandals ... and my self-respect. I shook it off my foot as the guy began to laugh. "Er ... and free ice cream with each ticket?" I bumbled. "I will literally give you *all* of these cones, *right now*, if you come back with me to buy a ticket."

He smirked. "I'm a volunteer. But I'll gladly trade you those cones for your number."

I blinked, hearing him but not listening ... because only now did I recognize the Happy Days T-shirt peeking out from his bomber jacket.

A volunteer since *when,* five seconds ago?

In all my time at Happy Days, I'd never seen this dude. Not once. I wanted to call BS, but I was also terribly afraid of making a mistake. He seemed nice, and at this point, I wasn't sensing any threat or bad intent. Especially since his eyes didn't leave my face, waiting for something. I had no idea what.

Suddenly, the swagger on the man's face melted. "Maybe that was a little forward." And he cracked a boyish grin. "Name's Aikan. I'm here to help."

He extended his hand, and on reflex, I extended mine ... with an ice cream cone balanced between each finger. I kept one for myself.

"Help would be great! I'm Samira Shaw! Welcome to the crew, Aikan! Thanks for coming out!" I shoved the cones into his hand, not bothering to ask if that was the kind of help he meant.

He looked at the ice cream cones, highly amused. But he took them. "Nice to meet you, Miss Shaw." A beat. "Are you going to answer that?"

I creased my brow, and then I realized my phone was ringing. I wiped my free hand against my jeans and pulled it out. Holy moly, it was Alla. Something must have been going down in Johannesburg if she was calling me *this* late.

"Excuse me." I smiled and turned away from Aikan as I answered.

"Who did you piss off this time?" My partner's drawl crawled through the phone and sat in my ear like a pissed-off spider. Alla sounded supremely bougie and unimpressed. As usual. She took her role as "bad cop" pretty seriously most of the time, and today was no different. I smirked.

"Uh-oh. Did you wake up on the wrong side of the coffin this morning, honey?"

"Very funny. Get your ass over here. We have a case."

I shoved the vanilla sprinkle cone into my mouth. Ah, sweet addiction. "Oh yeah? Where at?"

A long pause. "Just ... get down here."

Oh boy, sounded serious. I hung up and turned back to say bye to Aikan—but he was gone. I looked around, and after a frantic headcount, I breathed in relief. All the kids were still here. All the other volunteers, too. And the hamburgers, much to my wolf's relief. The charity barbecue and raffle endured.

Aikan, however, had vanished without a trace ... but weirdly enough, even as I walked out of the park, his gaze burned into my back.

5

FANGS AND FUR

ALATHIA

"You took your time," I said to Samira. I was waiting in the reception area for her. I couldn't think properly when I was in the next room with that body stapled to the wall. So tightly crossed were my arms that my hands were turning numb.

She smirked. "My special werewolf moonbeam transatlantic space-and-time-bender thingy was a little wonky today."

"What?"

Samira gave me a mysterious look, and I rolled my eyes. God only knows how that girl gets from the Bronx all the way to Jo'burg so quickly, and every time I ask, she spouts some cryptic answer that doesn't make sense. A different answer, actually, every time. Sometimes I think she just gets a kick out of messing with me.

"Shall we, my lady?" She lopes right by me before I can let her have it.

I feigned annoyance that she had kept me waiting, but truthfully I was happy to see her. It was impossible to dislike the werewolf shifter, and God knows we'd been through enough together to cement a deep and authentic relationship. We had seen each other at our best and our worst; revealed our real selves to each other, no filter. Just our genuine selves: flaws, fangs, and fur.

Living as a vampire behind the Masquerade, even in one of the most cosmopolitan cities in the world, can be a lonely existence. Plus, I don't play well with others. But Samira's different. She's dark-skinned and sweet-faced. Impossibly pretty, with eyes that shift from brown to gold. She has a fierce energy I've always admired. Whereas I feel I need to conserve my energy, Samira's always raring to go, ready to party, up for the game. You'd be forgiven for thinking she's a dumb puppy the first time you meet her, but you couldn't be more wrong. She's super-smart, with an excellent hunting nose. Her instincts are on point and she's loyal to a fault. In short, she's the best partner I could have imagined, and I was more than lucky to have her.

Couldn't let *her* know that, though.

"Are you wearing my eye shadow?" I asked. "And why do you smell like burnt caramel?"

Samira smiled. "None of your business!"

She was kidding, but I did see some emotion flash over her usually placid face. There was something she wasn't telling me.

"New boyfriend?" I ventured. She was clumsy with men and wore her heart on her sleeve. In my mind, it was a miracle she ever got laid.

Samira guffawed. "Girl, BYE. No way!"

"Well then," I said. "That makes two of us."

It took her a moment to comprehend what I had said, but then she frowned. "What? What about New Guy? He was totally nice. Emotionally available. Dressed well. Worked out. And was hot as Hades."

I sighed. *Emotionally available* was the problem. Damn humans and their constant desire to connect, when all I wanted was a good regular bang.

She didn't let it go. A dog with a bone. If you'll excuse the pun. "What was his name? Frank?"

"Old news," I said, not looking forward to wrestling with sleep again later in my cold bed, with a pillow that still smelled of him.

"But he was so *into* you," Sami said. "I could see it from a mile away."

"Exactly."

"Wait, don't tell me. You broke up with him because he was falling for you."

"I don't break up with humans. It's too messy."

Samira looked confused again, and then understanding dawned on her face. "Oh, Alla ... you *mesmerized him* into breaking up with you?!"

"It's a simpler solution," I said. "Cleaner."

"Sounds like baggage. And also like genius. Cold-hearted genius ... but genius."

"I'll take that as a compliment."

A smirk pulled at her lips. "As you should."

"Anyway, small talk about my dead heart and current dearth of lovers is not why we're here." I looked pointedly at the minuscule security camera in the corner of the ceiling of the reception room. "We've got bigger problems."

Like a psychopath with a grudge who knows where we work and how to breach our military-specced security system.

"I thought the system was supposed to be unbreachable," said Samira.

"So did I."

"And we pay BlackJack *how* much every month?"

"Too much," I said. "I called them. They're coming in tomorrow to investigate."

"Get a refund," said Sami, as if the money mattered.

I wasn't worried about the cash. I never worried about money. Despite my parents not leaving me a cent—and who could blame them, in their circumstances?—I've built up a small personal fortune over my extended lifetime. When you live for centuries, the compound interest really adds up. But Samira lives paycheck to paycheck. She wouldn't know a sound investment if it bit her on her furry ass. Sami was all about seizing the day. Fashion, make-up, accessories, gadgets? She was there waving her credit cards in the air and yelling, "*Carpe* freaking *diem!*"

One look at Samira on payday had commission-based salespeople in Sandton City salivating. And that was just her wardrobe. Her refrigerator at home got the same treatment. Come the last day of the month, you couldn't open the door of her fridge without a tray of lamb chops or a pack of bacon falling out. And it wasn't just her kitchen she stocked; she was forever buying groceries for the less fortunate, including gin for that grumpy old neighbor in that crummy apartment building of hers and dog food for the shelter on Koning street. It was as if money burned a big fat hole in her designer jeans, and she was perfectly okay with that. Until it was gone, of course.

"A refund is the least of our problems," I said.

Samira folded her arms. "Speak for yourself, Rockefeller."

"You'll see what I mean," I said, gesturing at the closed office door.

But Sami didn't move. In fact, as she looked at the door, her entire body tensed. Her wolf's hackles were already raised. Of course, she had already guessed that something nasty was waiting for her on the other side. I had a nose for blood, but Sami's sense of smell was more like a superpower.

She pulled a disgusted face. "I hoped I imagined that reek."

I shook my head. Forever the optimist, even when the sorry truth stared her in the face. Or wafted up her nose. Whatever.

Samira looked tentatively at the closed door and sniffed the air. "Male victim. Big spender. Two hours dead."

"Spot on," I said. All that through a door. I never knew how she did it.

"A lot of blood ... and ... something else. He was made to suffer."

I nodded. There was no more putting it off. I leaned past the Lycan and reached for the handle.

6

ONE HELL OF A MESSAGE

SAMIRA

I'D BEEN hungry all day, but this made me never want to eat dead meat again.

No wonder Alla hadn't wanted to meet me up here. Some sadistic psycho had had a great time playing a game of "Pin the Tail on the Vic" and apparently he'd had a freaking ball while doing it.

Except the "pins" were 8-inch nails ... and this? This was *not* a game.

Someone clearly held a grudge against this guy. And maybe us, too, considering that this was one hell of a message. But why?

As if activated by the question itself, all my senses began to dilate, allowing the information in the room to permeate my body, creating a mosaic of sound, scent, and sight. During this, my dear friend Alla disappeared, melting into what was becoming a mental golden web of sensory information ... and woven into that web was a story of blood and terror.

"There wasn't much of a struggle," I murmured. "Not in here, at least."

I extended my hand, and Alla tossed me a pair of gloves from our desk drawer. I slipped them on as I crouched down, still homed in on what my nose had already picked up.

"The dirt of the footprints is concentrated into firm bipedal impressions on the floor. Sandy loam, which is the kind of soil you have over here in Jo'burg. So the murder happened somewhere in this city. Not exactly an 'aha' moment, but really, the body could have come from anywhere."

I cocked my head as my nose picked up the faint scent of rubber. The scent's long trail ran across the office floor, from the door to the wall where the man hung. "Huh. Okay. The victim *also* left bipedal impressions, but they aren't concentrated, nor are they made of soil. They are rubber residue, two consistent lines of it." I traced my finger over one of them. "The victim was dragged across the threshold. And then impaled."

I leaned closer to the victim, much closer than I would have liked considering the foul gases that have just started to leak from his cavities. I sniffed, and though my stomach lurched in disgust, I somehow waded through the layers of smells on the man.

Underneath the scent of death was cologne. Christian Dior Sauvage, to be exact. The lingering moisture around his mouth told the tale of imbibed scotch, aged about 50 years, and chased with a few breath mints. That, and ...

I sniffed down the body, mentally marking each area with the brand name it was wearing. Versace Eros aftershave and deodorant to match. Smelled like this guy was either seriously metrosexual or about to go on a hot date.

For whatever reason, though, I couldn't pick up a scent around the midsection or under the arms, which is likely how the murderer would have carried him in.

Whoever did this was *good*. Scarily good. And his cleanup was even better.

But it was just inches farther south that I smelled something new, and I was so shocked by it that I shot up and stumbled back. Alla was already at my side, brandishing her pistol, ready to unleash hell.

"What is it?!"

Mouthing the words, disbelief had them locked in the back of my throat. Locked because the Masquerade had forbidden the very thing I'd just detected, so this couldn't be—it just wasn't possible—

"EARTH TO SAMI," Alla snarled, snapping her fingers in front of my face. "What's wrong?"

My eyes wide, the words looped in my mind, finally forming on my tongue: "Alla. I smell a *werewolf* on this guy. A Lycana, to be exact. And I smell her on his ... doodle."

7

AN AFFAIR WITH A WEREWOLF

ALATHIA

"His what?" I asked. I'm no prude, but Samira's words shocked me. Or rather, the implications shocked me.

She looked in my direction without really seeing me, her eyes clouded with whatever new information was swarming in her head.

"This could be bad news," she said, her voice trembling with a faint growl.

"*Could* be?" I said, blinking. "A werewolf nailed an expensive human to our office wall and you think it may or may *not* be a problem?"

"He wasn't killed by a wolf," said Samira.

"But you just said—"

"I said he had a date with a Lycan. Not all of us like to kill our conquests after mating."

"Depends how bad the date is," I said. It was a feeble attempt at a joke, but neither of us laughed. Samira was right; this murder wasn't a werewolf's style. God knows I had seen enough maimed bodies to know what a wolf's victim looked like.

"He's wearing more cologne than a fifteen-year-old virgin," said Samira. "And look at this." She pointed to a faint band of untanned skin on his ring finger.

"So he was having an affair?"

"Probably."

"An affair with a werewolf," I mused. "That's one way to keep life interesting."

Sami winced at the corpse. "If by 'interesting' you mean short and painful."

"How did he discover Lycana, I wonder?"

"Too late to ask," said Sami.

My latex gloves were still on. I stepped forward again and patted down the dead man. You'd think I wouldn't mind corpses, given my species, but they actually give me the creeps. I fought my instinct to recoil as I touched him, opening his jacket and rifling through his pockets. Neither of us was surprised to find an empty holster on his hip and a gold wedding band in his inner pocket. There was something else, though. A red lanyard with a chipped access card.

"Bingo," I said.

The card was blank, apart from a high-tech logo and the silver chip. Two letters, both Cs, just touching, and printed so that they looked 3-D. No name, no designation, just the symbol that seemed to hover in the air over the card.

Neither of us needed to say anything; we both recognized it right away. It was the logo of Crimson Corp, the South African-based multibillion-rand corporation that had helped bring peace to the country with its synthetic blood products, alongside other cutting edge product developments. We had Crimson Corp to thank for keeping the country's vampire population in check and the humans—relatively

—safe. Vamps had no excuse nowadays; they could feed on vegan blood straws all day long. We'd come a long way from the days of needing to attack hapless humans to keep our blood sugar from plummeting. Nowadays, it was only the very reckless who took their chances on the real thing. I won't lie, it was a daily struggle, especially when you have the aforementioned hapless humans in your bed, offering their bodies to you, and you can practically feel their blood pulsing beneath their warm skin.

"Alla?" said Sami. "You look a little pale. You want to sit down?"

I swallowed hard. It had been a long day. "I'm fine. Just thinking."

"What is there to think about?" asked Samira. "We've got his access card. Let's go."

We climbed into the purring Jaguar, and I shared the address of the Crimson Corp's headquarters with Edgar.

"Hey, Ed," said Samira. "How's the family?"

Sam knew more about my driver than I did. She knew all his kids' and grandkids' names, ages, and favorite hobbies. She was a natural talker and an avid listener, watching her in action made me feel exhausted. I sat back and practiced my resting bitch face while she and Edgar caught up.

"Is little Becky still a tomboy? Did Ron's team win the inter-house gala? And have you finished building that big old oak treehouse yet?"

They chatted as we drove, and I gazed out of the window, thinking of the dead man. I couldn't imagine what connection we had to him, but there he was, hanging in our office like a moth pinned to a board. I'd need to get a cleaner in. And a medical examiner to check out the body for anything we may have missed.

"What does Mikey want for his fifth birthday next week? Any ideas?"

"Anything to do with LEGO," Edgar said, his eyes twinkling in the rearview mirror. "Or *Star Wars*—"

"Edgar," I cut in. They both stopped talking. "There's a mess at the office."

He stopped smiling. "I thought there would be, Miss Laurent. I have the Cleaner on standby."

"Can he see to it tonight? The security people are coming in the morning."

"He cleared his schedule. He's just waiting for a green light."

"Ah, Edgar," said Samira wistfully. "You're worth your weight in gold, you know that? I wish I could clone you."

Edgar chuckled and accelerated out of a corner.

"Seriously," she said. "I'd do anything to have my very own Edgar."

"He'd be lucky to have you," said the driver, and I rolled my eyes, but not before making a note in my phone's calendar to have a massive LEGO Death Star set sent to Mikey on his birthday.

8

BATTERY LOVE

SAMIRA

"This is PIMP!"

Okay, I'd seen Crimson Corp in passing many times before, but somehow, tonight, it looked a million times more awesome. Its tallest tower, the one that housed the central offices, stood well over 1000 feet. It glowed with bright, warm lights, as though wearing a shawl of stars stolen from the night.

But that wasn't the best part. The rest of the company, and all its divisions, was built into its very own man-made mountain range. Not a huge one, but wide and vast and imposing enough to underscore Crimson Corp's dominance as a biotech company in both South Africa and throughout the world.

Plus, the location offered its employees and their families some great hiking and nature perks. And for the werewolf side of me, roaming perks, which I would now get to exploit. Illegally.

I pressed my face against the glass and almost rudely let out a doggish whine.

Alathia snickered. "Want me to open a window?"

Without looking away from Crimson Corp, I reached over my shoulder to give Alla the middle finger. Alathia laughed.

We pulled up to the bottom of one of the many hiking trails that led to and from the entrances of the company. A dozen ways in, and just as many ways out. The wolf in me loved it, but my logical human side knew that this was a hot mess waiting to happen. When anything could come from anywhere, we had a problem. Especially because we were about to break in.

From the backseat, I wrapped my arms around Edgar's neck and planted a kiss on his cheek. "Bye, Eddie!" And I jumped into the night. A second later, I heard Alathia follow less enthusiastically, but not before telling Edgar to keep out of sight and keep the car ready. He nodded and pulled off, and Alathia joined me on the trail.

"So?" she murmured. "You know where you're going?"

I smiled and nodded. Of course I did. I tilted my head back, closed my eyes, and took in a deep, calming breath to relax, to allow the melding of my two minds. When I finally opened my eyes, the rest of my senses opened too, and they drank in the night. My adrenaline spiked, and I knew the wolf was now taking the lead, mentally leashed only by the woman I'd just placed backstage.

I was ready to hunt.

Within minutes I found the most penetrable, hidden entrance to Crimson Corp and break out our lock-picking gear, and Alla and I were already hotly debating.

Of course, we were arguing about something that had *nothing* to do with our mission. Courtesy of me, the queen of distractions, dog stuff, and diss tracks.

"Alaaathia," I mocked. "Would *yooouu* do aaannnything for youuurrrr Edgaar?"

The sneer snaked from my mouth in an exact replica of Alla's snooty bitch voice. Well, almost exact, except I took it to a Queen Elizabeth level. Alla scoffed. She focused hard on calibrating the digital decryptions in front of her, but I kept talking. The *girl* in me kept talking, anyway. The wolf on the leash was the lookout, scanning the perimeter.

"Of course I wouldn't, Saahmiii," I continued, emphasizing her drawl. "Because *I*, the great vampire queen *Alaaathia*, think Edgar is a peasant, and *I* don't even really *caaare* that his foolish grandson likes LEEEEGOS."

Alla snorted at me but kept her gaze on the flying numbers on her screen. Even in the dark, I saw her smirk from the corner of my eye. "Just because you steal my make-up doesn't mean you can steal my Edgar," she muttered.

"He's not *your* Edgar. He's *our* Edgar."

"Oh? And do you pay for him to be '*our Edgar*'?"

"THAT'S COMPLETELY BESIDE THE POINT! The point is that you are unfairly possessive of a sweet old man that you don't even want in your flow like that—"

"In my ... what?"

"And this is just how you roll. Every time any guy gets close, you do your mind-bending thing and 'make' him break up with you or leave you. You don't even have the guts to do it yourself! You cringe at the idea of someone getting close to you, but then you want to be possessive of *Edgar*? Old-ass *Edgar*? You have some nerve!"

"Ugh. Sami ..." Alathia sighed, and I knew what she was going to say. I rolled my eyes and cut her off before she could even say it.

"My dear little Saahmiii, you are too young to understand the triaaals and tribulaaations of an old vaahmpiiire like me." With a melodramatic voice, I filled in the words for her. "You laack the experience of —yeah, I KNOW I was only born *this* century, but that doesn't stop me from loving people."

"Love is pointless. It doesn't actually do or mean anything, Sami. You'll learn that eventually."

"No. Love is like a battery. Just because it doesn't last doesn't mean it never worked."

She looked at me, chastened, maybe considering this as wisdom ... but suddenly, her face hardened again, perhaps thanks to an old memory. She fell back into herself, into a known darkness.

"Sure, kid," she muttered flatly. "Stick around long enough. Live long enough. Lose enough people. Then try to lecture me."

A happy beep cut through the night, followed by the faint *click* of the door's metal lock disengaging. Bingo, we were in. But I didn't rush inside immediately. I could smell the guards near the door and to keep it neat, I'd have to let Alla handle this one.

She stepped in, and as I predicted, the guards rushed her.

Then there was nothing but talking. Pleasant conversation, even.

"Your wives are cheating on you," Alla said, quite nonchalantly. "You should go home and handle that."

"My wife is cheating on me. I'm going home to handle that." The same sentence, parroted by two voices.

I hid behind the door as both guards casually walked out of the building. I looked at their hands. The idiots weren't even married, but okay.

I stepped into the building behind her and closed the door. The little light that had been coming in from outside vanished, leaving us in darkness.

"So anyway, as I was saying, I *have* lost people," I said, continuing our conversation. "Six people, to be exact. And none of them even wanted me. At least the people you push away *want* to be with you."

I didn't want to admit the pain that rode under that comment, but it was hard to ignore, and it got Alla's attention. She finally looked at me, her eyes pinched in sympathy.

"Oh, Sami."

"Forget it. It's not your fault, and I don't need you feeling bad for me. I'm just saying, maybe appreciate what you've got for a change ... not just when you're about to lose it."

I forced back the rest of my words and I breezed by her, walking deeper into the dark belly of Crimson Corp. I stopped and surveyed the massive foyer. It stretched out in front of us until it morphed into a black chasm of darkness that not even I could see through. But I could still smell through it, and no one else was here. At least not on *this* floor.

Alla pulled up next to me, unsure of what to say. Like me, she stared into the darkness. The silence between us was fat and awkward, like the bullied kid in class who ate too much cake.

My fault. I hadn't meant to come at her like that. It wasn't her fault I was abandoned as a pup. Not her fault I was born a runt. Not her fault my family thought me too weak to be worth anything. And also not her fault I envied that people actually *wanted* to be in her life. Funny, how each of us desired just what the other had: my solitude, her many admirers. Each came with a cost.

Still. I yearned for it anyway.

"Sorry," I muttered. "Let's just—"

"I appreciate *you*, Sami," she said. She wasn't allowing me to change the subject. Not yet. "And you're not going anywhere, right? How's *that* for battery love?" She was smiling, fangs gleaming in the night. Her smile was a rare thing, so it made me look at her.

I smirked. Immortal Arcanes like ourselves had "battery love." Sounded kind of kinky when you thought about it, but sure, it'd do. "Meh. It's fine, I guess."

Not *just* fine. The best. She was the sister I never had, and I knew it. More importantly, Alla knew it. So instead of talking about it further, we shared a smile and sallied forth, ready to catch some bad guys.

But first, I had to pee.

9

SHAKEDOWN

ALATHIA

"You're kidding, right?" We were in the middle of breaking into the headquarters of the biggest corporation in the country and she had to pee? How old was she? Two?

Sami scowled at me. "You wouldn't understand."

"You're right," I said. "I used the bathroom before our field trip. Like a regular grown-up."

I know I give the wolf a hard time, but was it too much to ask that she think ahead before we embark on illegal activities? Soon she'd say she's hungry. She'd complain about her blood sugar bottoming out. When would she learn to carry a protein bar around in her pocket? Especially when we're breaking and entering.

"All I want to do," I whispered at her, "is find the vic's office, have a look around, and get out. Can you hold it?"

In the dim light, Samira looked at me and shook her head. At least she had the grace to look apologetic. I clenched my jaw and motioned for her to keep walking. We'd find a bathroom, shake down the dead dude's den, and then get out. Of course, without the man's name, I didn't have a clue where to find his office, but Samira's sense of smell would lead us there. As much as she drove me crazy, I wouldn't be able to do this gig without her.

We crept along the sterile passage, subdued ceiling bulbs lighting our way, passing unmarked doors and empty rooms. Eventually, we came across the sign for a unisex bathroom and Sami darted inside while I stood sentinel. I was on high alert, pretty certain that we had tripped some kind of beam or missed a hidden camera on our way in. It had been way too easy. But between my manipulation skills and the revolver in my thigh holster, I was sure I could take care of any unforeseen problems. Still, anxiety tugged at my stomach. It was one thing getting myself into trouble, but if Sami ever got hurt, I'd never forgive myself. I silently tapped my feet, my silver-pointed boots flashing in the dim light. Where was she, anyway? She'd better not be checking her hair and make-up. I waited for another minute, and then another. Something was wrong.

My breath caught in my throat as I blurred toward the door, ready to unleash my particular brand of violence on anyone who dared to touch Samira. But as my hand touched the swing door, it was as if I tripped a light switch, and darkness flooded the passage.

The shock of the dark coupled with worry for Sami sent my adrenaline surging, and my body automatically readied itself to do battle. Pictures of the John Doe flashed in my head: the hands and feet nailed to the wall, the stained scissors, the blood graffiti. Then I heard them. In the pitch black, they swooped at me. Covering my gaping mouth with leather-gloved hands and forcing my arms behind me, sending pain shooting through my shoulders. They trussed my wrists with something small and light—a zip-tie?—and I screamed and kicked, but there were three of them, maybe four. Their combined strength subdued me. I wanted to call to Samira to warn her, but I was gagged and didn't know how to do that without alerting the guards to her presence. Instead, I let them lead me away from the bathroom door and hoped Sami would be able to find me.

I knew I was strong enough to snap the zip-tie, and then I'd be able to grab my gun, but these were innocent people. They were just doing their jobs. I reminded myself that, despite my fear, these weren't the bad guys. Or were they?

The lights flickered back on and I looked at my captors. Five guards wearing high-tech protection and night-vision visors, which explained how they rushed at me, finding me immediately despite the dark. Fortunate for them, and unfortunate for me, because mesmerization doesn't work through night-vision lenses. I felt a grudging respect for them. They clearly knew what they were doing.

Two of the guards waited outside the bathroom while the other three pushed me along, away from Samira.

"Where are you taking me?" I asked.

The man jostling my right elbow just grunted in response. I wasn't expecting an answer, and I didn't get one.

10

GOOD DOGGY SHIT

SAMIRA

It took a minute to get away from Alathia's bitching. *You should have used the bathroom before we left!* Yeah, sure, but *she* didn't have the burden of dealing with my human bladder *and* the wolf's phantom urge to mark every new territory she saw.

And the closer the full moon got, the stronger that urge became.

If I didn't relieve those instincts as they arose, well ... there'd be some very, shall we say, feral consequences to deal with. Runt or not, just like any other Lycana, I gave new meaning to the word "bitch" when the full moon was at hand.

I sighed in relief, and so did my other organs as my bladder emptied. I washed my hands—okay, admittedly, I had little time for that, but the human side of me couldn't abide anything else. Just because wolves were related to dogs didn't mean we had to be—

My ears perked up as I heard the unmistakable sound of scuffling boots. The sounds were farther down the hallway, but they were getting closer by the second, and they'd be on Alla another second later. I moved toward the swing door and reached—when a black-gloved hand shot out from a stall and grabbed my wrist mid-air.

A body slunk from the shadows of the stall. As it did, my heart stopped, as much from pure shock as from my realization that someone had been in the bathroom the entire time. Lurking.

"What the ..."

His grip on me tightened. In the dark, his face remained a mystery. *Not human.* That's all my brain could manage as I realized I couldn't even detect him. He had no smell, no sound ... not even a heartbeat.

With his other hand, he reached behind him and locked the bathroom door. Oh crap.

My blade arced through the air. He blocked me, catching my other wrist, but I lashed out with a kick. He grunted and I high-kneed him in the face as he went down.

Freed as he slammed into the bathroom door, my eyes widened when it didn't budge. Alla probably heard that, and she was going to come in here, but she needed to get away—

"ALLA, RUN!" I screamed, hoping she'd hear me.

He tackled my midsection, and pain crackled through my back as we hit the opposite wall. I drove my blade into his shoulder—and I gasped as it *broke* on impact.

What the ...

But he'd already gotten his second wind. He was stronger than me—this being—this non-human thing that had no smell—

He grabbed my hair and threw me into the rows of mirrors above the trough sink. I yelped as I felt the glass spider-web on impact, as parts of my body crunched inward. I collapsed onto the trough, broken.

Before I could get up, he was on me, his grip at my neck and a gun in my face.

"Move again," he snarled. "And I'll pump you so full of silver that miners will be *begging* to get into your funeral."

His voice was low and husky, and he was not playing around. I could smell the horrid acidic burn of the silver bullets emanating from the gun. One shot would kill me, my regenerative powers be damned. I gritted my teeth.

"Who are you?" I growled. "What do you want?"

"You, Samira."

I curled my lip in disgust. If this guy was looking for a nighttime romp, he had another think coming. That ... and how did he know my name? I guess he registered the disgust in my face because he let me go and took a measured step back.

"Guess that was a little forward."

I blinked and slowly sat up. "What the ... *Aikan?*"

The man stepped into a shaft of moonlight. It *was* Aikan. He wasn't wearing his Happy Days shirt, and if he were, I'd think he was joking. Dude didn't look happy by a long shot. In fact, he looked wilder and more rugged than before, still hot-blooded after our fight. Sharp, handsome features I hadn't noticed in the plain light of day were highlighted now as he stared at me. Hard.

"Sorry to rough you up. It's ... not how I envisioned this conversation going."

"Really? You didn't expect that I'd trip out if you attacked me from a bathroom stall?"

He flashed me a smile. Maybe I was wrong, but he looked a bit lupine. "Arguably, I didn't attack you. You attacked *me*—"

"What the hell are you doing here? Why are you following me? How'd you even get to Jo'burg; are you a stalker?"

I got in his face as I interrogated him, but the sudden sizzle at my hip forced me back. He was still holding the silver-loaded gun, and therefore, the power. He reminded me of that as he kissed my hip with his Beretta.

"Down, girl," he muttered.

I growled. I *hated* it when people said that kind of "good doggy" shit to me. It always sounded prejudiced and condescending. Before I succumbed to the urge to rip the shit out of him, I turned my thoughts to what was really important.

"I need to go. Alla's in danger."

"So are *you*, Samira." And finally, Aikan holstered his weapon. "And if you don't listen to what I have to say, the rest of the world will be, too."

11

NOT MY CROWD

ALATHIA

The brutes shoved me around a couple of corners and then pushed me into an elevator, the space crowded with testosterone and bad haircuts. I breathed through the waves of panic that crept up my throat, reminding me of my centuries-old claustrophobia. The steel handrail dug into my back as I tried to create space between the sweating human bodies and my cool skin. The elevator took forever to reach the top of the skyscraper, and when the doors slid open, I couldn't hide my relief. I was happy to be let out, even if the guard at my elbow was a bit rough. I yanked my elbow away from him, irritated by his firm grip and bossy demeanor, but he just grabbed me again. I looked at him, taking in every detail. Beady eyes, bulbous nose, wiry eyebrows. I committed his features to memory so that if he harmed me at all, I could easily find him and ... even the score. I guess some people might call that vengeful, but I see it as righting the wrongs in the world. If a man hurts a woman, you can bet your bottom dollar I'll be there to hurt him right back. If this particular grub decided to harm me, he'd best start sleeping with his eyes open.

Within moments of reaching the top floor, we were standing outside a set of vast double-doors polished to within an inch of their lives.

Expensive paintings hung on the wall, framed in gold, as well as certificates and photographs. A tall man in a beautiful suit was shaking the president's hand in one of the pictures, having tea with a spiritual leader in another, and handing out candy to a sea of smiling young faces in what looked like Diepsloot or Soweto.

Ha, I thought. *As if CEOs ever really give a damn about kids mired in poverty.*

Still, you couldn't blame the guy for the PR. Every company has to do it, and to be fair, Crimson Corp does more for the country than any other corporation in South Africa. Without their synthetic blood we'd have a paranormal civil war on our hands, and the last time that happened it did not end well.

One of the guards stepped forward and rapped on the door. The guards seemed nervous; I could smell it in their breath and sweat. What were they scared of?

"Enter!" came a call through the shining timber.

The uniform pulled off my gag and leaned against the door, swinging it open and holding it to allow the rest of us to move inside. I'd expected a pimped-out office, but what I saw took my breath away. The office was glass on all sides, and gave the feeling of standing in outer space, with a carpet of city lights below and a crown of stars above. The clear night air all around us was the most beautiful shade of nothing I'd ever seen.

Holy wow, I wanted to say, but I held my tongue. I didn't want the man to think I was impressed by him. Just because he had a lot of money—okay, an absolute freaking fortune—didn't make him a person worthy of my respect. He stood up from behind his mahogany monstrosity of a desk and smiled at me. I wanted to take a step back, but I felt frozen in place. He walked over to me and dismissed the guards with the slightest nod of his head. Seemingly relieved, they scampered away, and as they did, so the tension in the room dissipated. That is, until he came right up to me. I took in his height—not many men are taller than me—his lunar skin, and the strong body I sensed through his stylish threads. As soon as our eyes met, I knew what he was. My body was on instant high alert.

"Ms. Laurent." He had a great voice. Warm, with an elegant accent.

"Call me Alathia."

"Alathia," he said, and his lips curved into a hint of a smile. "I've heard a great deal about you."

Somehow I doubted that. The kind of people someone like this guy hangs around with are moguls; CEOs and CFOs of Fortune 500 businesses and the top ten Johannesburg Stock Exchange companies. They were drinking Cristal at country clubs and exclusive cigar lounges where everyone slapped them on the back and laughed at their crap jokes. Not my crowd.

"I'm Damon Sullivan," he said. We didn't shake hands; it was not the vampire way. But I did appreciate him introducing himself. Of course, I knew his name—it was as much of a household name as milk or bleach—but one of my pet peeves is people who are so self-important they expect everyone to know who they are.

"Pleased to meet you," I said. "Even if this meeting is rather unexpected."

"Yes," he said, looking amused. "When one breaks into a building one doesn't expect to be offered champagne by its owner."

He swaggered to the corner of the room where he had a chilled bottle waiting for us, a white linen napkin draped over its neck, and pulled it out of its arctic water.

"No, thanks," I said.

What was he playing at?

He looked disconcerted for a moment, but then returned it. The ice crunched under the weight of the bottle as he wedged it back into the bucket.

"Do you offer overpriced drinks to all your captives?" I asked, and gestured at the zip-tie that was still binding my wrists together.

"Oh," he said, with a hint of remorse. He looked down at the drinks tray and picked up the bottle opener. He flicked open the small blade and came over to me. Before I even registered what was happening, he had cut the tie and in front of me again, the feeling of his touch lingering on my skin. Surrounded by the sparkling black sky, I looked into his eyes again. It was so surreal; it felt like we were the only two people in the universe.

"Might we get down to business?" he asked.

12

A NOBLE SUBMISSION

SAMIRA

"WHAT DO YOU MEAN, the world's in danger? What kind of Saturday morning cartoon tomfoolery is this?" I crossed my arms, no longer caring if this guy had the upper hand. I was done playing his games.

Aikan breathed in deeply, which told me he was questioning whether or not he should trust me. Guess he decided he had to because then he started to speak.

"That Doe in your office. His name is Benedict Jama. He was a good man, and he didn't deserve what happened to him."

My eyes widened. "How did you—did you kill him?" I remembered the map of suffering the murderer left on the victim's body, and suddenly I was pissed off again. The hairs on my body rose, and the wolf finally stirred, ready for round two. A round she was determined to win.

"No," Aikan said smoothly. "And even if I did, that's actually beside the point. Like I said: the world is in danger. And I don't mean in a mustache-twirling Dr. Dastardly sort of way. I'm talking about an extinction-level event of epic proportions. Extinction of the Arcanes themselves. *Our* extinction."

Our?

I creased my brow, stepped a little closer, and sniffed. He didn't *smell* like werewolf ... not exactly, anyway. More like simple soap. Maybe with patchouli?

I crept even closer. He didn't move. I continued to sniff—wait, what *was* this guy? —I even rose up on my tiptoes to examine his face. The sharp eyes that stared back at me were dark and brooding, but when I looked more closely, I could finally see them: flecks of shining gold and amber. The sprinkle of metallic color was revealed only for a split second after he blinked, but it was there.

Holy gosh sauce. He *was* a werewolf. Some other sort of werewolf, maybe, but definitely one of ours, and—

"GAH!" I stumbled back as he suddenly rubbed his nose on mine, *nuzzling* me. I shrieked and manically rubbed my nose. He started laughing. Uproariously.

"YOU JUST *KISSED* ME, YOU BASTARD!" I snarled.

"The wolf kissed you, not me."

"SAME DIFFERENCE!"

He smirked. "What's the big deal? Was it your first one?"

"IT DOESN'T MATTER IF IT WAS OR WASN'T! I DIDN'T GIVE YOU PERMISSION!"

He flashed me a grin, framed by slightly elongated canines. "Hey, *you* were the one being weird. Maybe you should consider yourself lucky. You of all people know what happens when you stare a werewolf in the eyes. I was well within my rights to attack you. Challenge me like that again, and I will."

"I wasn't challenging you! I was just—"

"Apology accepted, sweetheart."

I growled, and this time, I really *was* thinking about tearing his throat out, but he stepped forward, his eyes serious again.

"Samira. Crimson Corp is going to ask you and Alathia to take Benedict Jama's murder case. I suspect they'll want it wrapped up in-house, quietly. But you need to be careful around them. They're into some really bad shit—linked up with some bad people—and I'm afraid that Jama's death is just the beginning. That's why I need you to do me a favor."

Still grumbling and wiping my nose, I was listening. "What?" I growled.

"When you catch the criminal, *if* you catch him first, you need to deliver him to me. Not to Crimson Corp."

"Are you out of your mind? This is a murder case, not an episode of *The Punisher*. We deliver him to the cops. Period."

"This is different, Samira. You have to believe me."

"Why? Why should I believe anything you say? I don't even know you."

"But you know *them*," and as he said this, he shoved something in my face. His phone, glowing faintly in the moon-drenched darkness, played a video.

I creased my brow at the figures on the screen. A figure, twice the size of an NBA player and broader than two quarterbacks, lay on its side in an alleyway. It trembled under the veil of night, and I heard labored breathing. The sound of panting. Anyone else wouldn't have recognized the shape in the darkness, but I could.

A werewolf.

Moreover, its belly was swollen and distended. As something moved inside it, the wolf whined, its lupine howl carrying a heavy overtone of pain and suffering. She whined again, this time more desperately—

and my throat closed as I watched the first pup's red and slimy head ooze out of the wolf's loins.

GROSS.

It was a horrible bloodbath, and even I, a werewolf who was used to the sound and sight of blood, recoiled. Tearing into prey was one thing. Watching a birth was something different entirely.

As the wolf continued to whine and whelp, and the pups came one after another, I turned my eyes away. "Why are you showing me this?"

"Look again."

I did, just in time to see the wolf licking and eating the fluids and placenta off the pups. To the one buried in the middle, she gave special, gentler care. She nuzzled it, trying to encourage it to rush to a teat as her other four had just done. The pup was the smallest amongst all five of her litter. The runt. As it finally raised its scruffy black head into the moonlight, eyes shut but sniffing curiously, my gaze filled with tears.

It was *me*.

My blade was already at Aikan's throat.

"WHO ARE YOU?!" I screamed. Tears, now flowing freely, burned down my face. He didn't know the wound he'd just salted. "HOW DID YOU GET THIS?!"

"Calm down, Samira. The security guards might hear you."

"ANSWER ME!"

"My team can hack into pretty much any closed-circuit surveillance system we need to, given we have good reason."

He lowered the phone and stepped in closer, so close I could feel his heat. He walked right into my blade, indifferent to the thin beads of blood it drew from his neck. He stood a clean foot taller than me, but he poured his gaze into mine, as though to level our differences. I stared back defiantly, no longer caring if he took it as a challenge.

"What 'good reason' did you have for tracking my family? For tracking *me*?"

"A trade."

I started, a gasp in my throat.

"I know quite a bit about you, Samira," he continued. "Not everything. But enough. I know even more about your family. If you're interested, I'd like to share that information with you."

"But only if I deliver Jama's murderer." My knowing growl didn't sound very acquiescent, but it didn't seem to bother Aikan.

"Exactly. You can choose not to, of course, but then I'll give you nothing. That ... and we'd be on opposing sides of a very deadly fight. And if what I've seen tonight is any indication of your skills, it is a fight you'd surely lose."

"Are you threatening me?"

"I don't need to. It didn't take much for me to thrash you just now, and I was barely even trying. And even at full strength, you are still just a runt, after all."

He had some nerve pulling rank when he barely even registered as a werewolf himself.

"Newsflash," I snapped. "You might not have been using your full strength, but neither was I." I folded my arms and looked away. "I need to find my partner. She's in danger." Then I glared back at him. "Please move."

"Your partner is fine. She's been taken to the CEO's office."

He lifted his phone again, and clicking a button, changed the video playback to a different scene. A super plush and posh office that actually looked like a swanky sitting room more than an executive suite. Alathia was sitting across from a well-dressed man, her legs crossed, vengefully ignoring the drink in front of her. From her body language, I could tell she was pretty pissed, but the man across from her didn't seem to mind. He leaned back, enjoying his drink and whatever monologue he was giving her. One that she was clearly ignoring.

"Alla!" My insides lurched at the thought of her being trapped with this wannabe Don Juan. I needed to get to her. I straightened up.

"She's fine," Aikan insisted. "He's about to make her—both of you—an offer to take the case. The guards have just left to look for you. You need to let them find you, and, of course, act like this never happened."

I huffed. "Sorry to kill your master plan, Stan, but FYI? Alla is going to want to take the murderer into the cops. Not hand him over to some weird vigilante werewolf and his crew of uncanny a-holes."

"Then I guess you will have to go freelance on this one. Strike out on your own, so to speak. Quietly."

"What you're asking me to do is betray her, betray my *partner*."

"I'm asking you to save humanity ... and to trust me."

"Why in God's name would I trust *you*?"

"You already do, apparently. You might have killed me if you'd let the wolf take control, but you didn't," he says, looking me over. "So if you don't trust me, then why didn't you fight back for real? Why didn't you try to hurt me?"

It was true. I *could* have killed him if I'd wanted. In human form, I was weaker than him, but as a runt, I could also shift whenever I wanted. An ability only runts possessed, and our only real defence mechanism against the world ... and against other werewolves. Especially alphas like Aikan.

"I care about people," I said. "The werewolf doesn't. I have to remain in control, or people will die. Has nothing to do with trust. It's about honor, about keeping innocents alive and away from our world."

"That's a noble position to take. Especially for an Arcane who will always be feared—hunted—by the very people she aims to protect."

"So? You're clearly not human either, but you want to save the world anyway."

"Because I live in it." He hesitated and then smiled. "And now, because I know *you* live in it too."

Blood rushed to my cheeks, and for a moment, I didn't know what to say. Who *was* this psycho, anyway?

He moved in as if to tell me. Suddenly, his body was leaning against mine, and his fingers were sliding around my lower back, and for a moment, I was afraid he really *was* going to try something—that is, until I felt him slip his phone, the same one with the video of my mother on it, into my back pocket. His fingers lingered, only for a second, but I noticed. Even harder to ignore was how I *wanted* them to.

Down, girl.

"I'll be in touch," he murmured. Then he took a step back. "Take care of yourself, Samira. And, as I said ... keep this conversation to yourself."

In the next moment, he was through the bathroom door and gone, dissipating into the night just as quietly as he'd come. And yet, I could still smell him on my neck, feel him on my skin, hear those words in my ear: his soft promises of things to come ... and I had a feeling that his information on my family was just the beginning.

13

PIN THE TAIL ON THE DONKEY

ALATHIA

WE SAT at the vast boardroom table he had at the southeast part of his office, but not before Damon Sullivan had poured me a decent drink. Single malt whiskey, one block of ice, in a tumbler so pretty it deserved its own plinth in a crystal gallery. He placed it on the polished timber in front of me, the smell of peat and the walnut assailing my nose. I could have really gone for a drink then, but I held back. I needed a clear head if I was going to navigate this odd situation. I didn't know what the man's intentions were, and I didn't know where Samira was, either. Had she escaped? Had she been caught?

Damon registered the concern on my face.

"Your partner will not be harmed," he said. "Our intention is the opposite. We'd like to help you."

I crossed my arms and rested them on the table, thinking of the way I had been tackled and gagged. "We don't need your help."

"That is a pity," Damon said. "I was hoping we could help each other."

"Who's the dead guy in our office?" I asked.

Pain flickered over his face. He either knew and liked the John Doe or he was a very good actor. I saw him swallow hard as if to stave off the emotion he was feeling, and then he cleared his throat and looked into my eyes.

"His name was Benedict Jama. He was a good man, and a loyal employee." Damon looked out of the huge plate glass window beside us. "He didn't deserve to die. And he certainly didn't deserve to die like that."

"Like what?" I said, angling my head at him.

Damon slid his hand into his inner pocket and brought out a piece of paper. He unfolded it and placed it on the table between us. It was a small square photograph of the John Doe—Benedict Jama—nailed to my formerly tasteful wallpaper.

"How did you get that?" I asked.

"It was emailed to me from an address that doesn't exist."

"How did you know it was taken in our office?"

"I didn't. But then you two showed up here with his access card. It wasn't difficult to put two and two together."

"We wanted to search his office," I said. "We need to know who did this to him and why they thought our office was a good place to play 'pin the tail on the donkey. The sadistic version.'"

"You could have asked," he said. "Made an appointment. Come through the front door."

"Right," I said, sarcasm adding a snarl to my voice.

"But you didn't," he clasped his hands together and leaned forward on the table. "And that's what I like about you two."

"You like that we break the law?"

"I like that you don't ask permission. That you take what you need. That you don't give a damn who I am or how much money I have."

"I have my own money," I said.

"I know. I did a thorough background check on both of you."

"Of course you did."

I didn't even want to know what he had uncovered. My criminal record is more checkered than a chessboard. It was one of the few downsides to being extremely good at my job. It usually didn't hinder me ... much.

I looked at my watch. Where the hell was Samira? I eyed my drink, which I had yet to touch, despite my thirst and the delicious aroma of it.

"I saw that the Laurent bloodline originally comes from Croatia," he said. "I find it quite interesting that—"

"I don't talk about my family," I said, and he stopped mid-sentence.

Damon Sullivan lifted his hands and showed me his palms. "Forgive me. I didn't mean to—"

"Let's stick to business, shall we? You want to hire us to find Benedict Jama's killer."

"Er," he said. "Yes."

"And you'll give us everything we need to begin the investigation."

"Yes. And five hundred thousand rand."

I hoped my face didn't give away my surprise. Usually, I had to play hardball with customers, doubling their initial fee offer and then negotiating down to slightly more than they ever intended to pay. I was planning to start with two-fifty and settling on two. Sullivan was offering double my original—inflated—asking price.

"Sounds reasonable," I said, trying to keep my voice even. I could do with a small capital injection, I guess. I had a security system to fix, and old Edgar probably deserved a raise. The truth was, I didn't need the money ... but Samira certainly did. That was when I heard something outside.

"Ah," said Damon, smiling. "The wolf is at the door."

14

AFFIRMATIVE ASS-KICKING

SAMIRA

Ugh, boooooriiinnng.

Mostly because I didn't fight the guards as they dragged me through the complex and finally dumped me into the CEO's office. After Aikan left, it hadn't been that hard to find them, pretend to be startled, and then "put up a fight" before I allowed them to subdue me and take me into custody.

I dropped to the velvety floor of the CEO's office, and the door had barely closed behind me before he started in.

"Ah! The legendary Samira Shaw! So pleased that you could join us. I am Damon Sullivan, CEO of Crimson Corp."

The man's voice was as smooth as silk and as calm as summer rain. Seemed like the type that wasn't surprised by much. Rather like Alathia. Also, like Alathia, he was as pale as the full moon, tall, and of course, flawless and beautiful.

"Yeah, thanks for the invite," I muttered dryly as I stood up and brushed myself off. I looked around as I did so, tried to remain unimpressed by his stature, but it was a hard task.

"I've heard great things about you," he continued. "*Both* of you. I've very much been looking forward to meeting you in the flesh. I hoped such a meeting would be under more ... pleasant circumstances, as it were, but alas. Here we are."

"Yeah," I said. "Of course. Pleased to meet you, *and* your jackbooted thugs, 'as it were.'" That last part came out snippy and snooty, and he raised his eyebrows, amused.

"I assure you," he purred. "The pleasure is all mine."

Chyeah, seemed like it. He looked *just* like the type of sexy slick-talking playboy who'd take everything from you, your bank account, and your willing body while giving absolutely nothing back.

A vampire ... in every sense of the word.

The age-old rivalry between our races threw my blood into a simmer and I narrowed my eyes at him. I couldn't help it, really. To dislike most vampires on sight was literally bred into most were-wolves, and I'd done everything possible to deprogram myself of my prejudice. Except when they attacked me, or my friends, like this guy had.

But when Alathia whipped around and glared at me, I shrank back. My blood cooled even as her gaze consumed my body in a hellish visual firestorm. She wanted to rip me to pieces ... maybe for worrying her, or maybe for leaving her to the wolves (excusing the pun). Either way, she wasn't happy with me.

I offered her a nervous smile as I sat down in one of the chairs Damon had shown me. Still determined to be a bitch, though, I sat several feet away from both of them and crossed my arms.

"Ms. Laurent was just explaining to me the reason for your late-night visit," he said while smiling and pouring an expensive-looking whiskey into a glass.

"You mean you were holding her hostage," I snapped back. I bristled as I got to my feet again, ready to scrap. "And that ends *now*."

"Not at all, Miss Shaw. I offered your partner the opportunity to depart minutes ago. She all but insisted that she wait for you to join us. We've come to some mutual conclusions that I believe will interest you."

I gave him a look that clearly said I didn't buy his BS, but my whirlwind of semi-violent thoughts suddenly calmed as he stared at me … more with a clinical eye than with attraction. His very gaze was a scalpel on my body.

"*What?*" I snapped. "And don't tell me you have a lazy eye, either."

He chuckled, genuinely amused. "Just observing, Miss Shaw."

"You know what they say about staring a werewolf in the eyes." Aikan's very true words leaped off my tongue; each one cracked a real warning in the air. "It'll get you into a lot of trouble."

He smirked, and I see the cockiness under his genteel veil. "My apologies. It's just that I rarely get to see one of you so very close up. And so close to the full moon."

"One of me. Maybe if you hadn't run us underground, you'd get to see us as often as you liked," I snapped. The real truth of it put a growl in my voice, and I didn't bother hiding it.

More progressive Arcanes often wondered about the conflict between the Orders Chiroptin and Lupine, but for me, it was simple, laid bare in a history that repeated over and over. Both Orders looked human, but one of us didn't turn into bloodthirsty ravaging monsters every month. As such, the Old World vampires had used their ability to blend in with the humans to launch a drip campaign; they'd planted Chiroptin *everywhere*: in the film industry, in publishing, in every media outlet possible, from where they ruled the humans with a glamorized iron fist.

Their propaganda eventually convinced the world that vampires, whether fictitious or real, were "sexy" and "desirable." Meanwhile, all we got was #TeamJacob and a bunch of doggy jokes. But that wasn't enough to erase the bloodthirsty stigma we had on our reputations. Ironic, as we consumed less human blood per capita worldwide than vampires did.

Still, in their manipulation of the human experience, the vampires convinced the humans to hunt us, kill us, wipe us out. Meanwhile, they got to sit back, blend in, and make fat stacks, all while increasing their influence in the world ... and diminishing ours.

At my accusation, though, Damon didn't flinch. In fact, he looked cowed.

"A centuries' old wrong, Miss Shaw," he admitted. "Which I, and my company, endeavor every day to rectify. We all do." He was speaking for his kind now, and I vehemently disagreed. But I didn't interrupt.

"That is precisely why we actively engage in fostering diversity and intercultural fellowship here at Crimson Corp," he continued. He beamed brightly, *so* proud of himself. "We *just* launched a brand new affirmative action program designed specifically for the integration of persons of Lupine descent—"

"Wolves don't need affirmative action. We just act ... in the affirmative. Affirmative ass-kicking, to be exact."

He was unshaken by my threat, and by now, Alathia was cutting her eyes at me from across the room.

"I am pleased to hear that, Miss Shaw," he said. "It makes me all the more confident that you will fulfill our contract and bring Mr. Jama's murderer to justice."

His words pressed the "pause" button on my smart mouth, and I looked at Alla, mouth agape. "Excuse me?"

"We're taking the job, Samira," Alla said. And she didn't sound open to discussion either. "And we're starting tonight."

15

A FEW FRIES SHORT OF A HAPPY MEAL

ALATHIA

Samira scowled at me, but I didn't care. If she had used the bathroom at home, she wouldn't have missed out on half of this meeting. What took her so long in there, anyway? Fixing her hair? High impact mascara? Glitter eyeshadow? She did seem to have a kind of mad glint in her eye. What was that about? All the while I was worried about her, thinking something bad had happened.

She simmered with fury, and waves of angry heat radiated from her. Werewolves are so damn emotional. They act before they think. Have you ever heard of the Werewolf EQ test? No? Exactly. That's because it doesn't exist. The wolves would have eaten the whole bag of marshmallows and the instructor before anyone had time to spell "emotional intelligence."

"I'm pleased you'll be taking the case," said Damon, and I sensed that Samira wanted to kick me under the table.

"We're not doing it for you," I said. I finally took a sip of the single malt, and the amber liquid burned my mouth. The second sip was smooth and smoky; beach bonfire and ash. I tasted the oak barrel, the oiliness, the hint of walnut.

Samira, following my lead, threw the liquor down her throat and slammed her tumbler on the table. Damon Sullivan looked amused again. A tot from that bottle cost around a month's worth of Samira's rent and she had just shot it like cheap tequila at a Mexican piñata party. The woman had chutzpah, that's for sure. I wondered what the lupine version of chutzpah would be.

"We're not doing it for you," I said again. "We're not even doing it for the poor bastard who was murdered. We're doing it is because he was nailed to our wall. I don't like the idea that a psychopath thinks he can come and go as he pleases, especially when he's in the habit of stapling people to our wallpaper."

"Fair enough," said Sullivan.

"Also, if this killer is targeting Crimson Corp, we'll have a much bigger problem on our hands."

The CEO and the werewolf both blinked at me.

"You think they're targeting this company?" asked Samira. Then in a low voice, she grumbled, "Maybe we should just leave the killer to it, then."

"*I have a hunch,*" I said, raising my voice over her snide comment. I looked at Damon. "You're the CEO of the most successful business in the country—"

"—on the continent, actually," he said.

Sami rolled her eyes.

"So I'm assuming you have some enemies?" I said. "Corporate espionage? Blackmail? Extortion?"

Damon frowned at me. "Crimson Corp is a well-respected business," he said. "The Arcanes know that without our products, a violent civil war would break out. The vampires—"

I didn't need a lecture about how synthetic blood products had brought relative peace to the Masquerade. Yes, Crimson had revolutionized the way vampires lived, and spared a shit ton of humans' lives. Yes, it had ensured the safety of the dwindling vampire population. Without vampire attacks, the vampire hunters stayed home and bottled peaches, or whatever it is that out-of-work vamp slayers did. I had no doubt that if the attacks were ever to begin again, the hunters would brandish the wooden stakes from under their pillows and rally the pitchfork crowds.

I interrupted him. "I know the *stakes*," I said, and only just managed not to crack a smile at the pun. "All I'm saying is that everyone has enemies."

"Especially CEOs of multibillion-rand enterprises," said Samira.

We stared at Sullivan, who put his drink down. "There is someone."

Sami and I both sat up a little.

"I thought he was harmless," said Damon. "Up until recently—"

"Who is he?" I asked.

Damon smiled and shook his head. "I thought he was just one of those guys, you know? Those ex-military conspiracy theorist doomsday prepper guys who get some kind of hint of what lies beyond the Masquerade and then spend their lives chasing the pot of gold at the end of the rainbow. In my experience, they're usually harmless. But this guy refuses to give up. He's always calling us, telling us he knows what we're doing here. Knows about the Arcanes. Knows 'what's behind the curtain.' Threatens to tell the international press, the police, the bloody Illuminati."

Sullivan stood up and sauntered over to his desk, picking up his sleek silver laptop and bringing it back to the boardroom table. He tapped a few keys and then turned the screen so that we could see it. It was a security camera clip of a man creeping around the exterior of the

Crimson Corp building. He was in full military gear, dark gray camouflage pants, sturdy black boots, and what looked like a bullet-proof vest. He had a rifle slung over one arm and a camera around his neck. There was also something in his right hand, a slim can.

"Then a week ago, just before Benedict went missing, he shows up with a backpack of explosives. Threatened to blow the building sky-high if we didn't stop what we were doing right away. If we didn't come clean and tell the world about the supernatural creatures we were harboring."

The prepper had a manic look about him, and his eyes were wild. Drugs, maybe. Or fear. Then he approached the security camera and held the tin up to the lens, and the visual turned black.

Samira whistled. "That guy's clearly a few fries short of a Happy Meal."

Sullivan rewound to the clearest picture of his face and paused the video.

"His name is Malcolm Beukes. I'll text you his address."

"You know his address?" asked Samira. "Why haven't you sent the cops over?"

"I did. They said there was no evidence of terrorist activity."

"What about the backpack of explosives?" asked Samira.

Damon pursed his lips. "They were cans of spray paint."

"So he's not a real threat," I said. "He's a nuisance. All bark, no bite."

Samira cast me a sharp look.

"You asked if I had any enemies," said Damon. "Malcolm Beukes has been threatening my company, my employees, and my safety for months." He glanced at his laptop screen again, where Malcolm's demented face glared back at us. "But he's not the only one."

16

DOGGY JOKES AND COLD SHOULDERS

SAMIRA

So I WAS BEING PETTY, sure. But I was also *pissed*.

I was upset at Alla, yes, but I was even angrier with myself. I'd been so worried about not telling her about Aikan or his little side mission; I'd cared what she thought, how it'd affect her. But oh, that didn't stop *Alla* from doing what Alla thought was best, without even consulting me! Alla and I were a team; how could she make these decisions without me? I mean, come on, the shady soul-sucking CEO did a little drink pouring and smooth talking, and suddenly *I* was the one on the outside looking in? What *I* thought didn't matter? *I* was in the dog house?

The wolf in me growled at the self-directed insult. Like I said: we wolves got nothing from dealing with vampires except doggy jokes and cold shoulders.

All these angry thoughts rattled through my brain as I jogged through the night. *Alone*. Despite Alathia's protests, I had refused to take the car with her. I mean, I loved her to pieces, and so did the wolf (when it wasn't hungry). Still, her forming a team with her vampy billionaire dream hunk really rubbed my fur the wrong way.

That, and the CEO's list of potential suspects that he somehow *magically* produced out of nowhere.

"Oh and byyyy the waaaaay," he'd drawled. "Here are some oooother ennnntities that you might want to ... look innnnto."

And then he'd just presented us with a list of his enemies: old-school vamps who hated that Crimson Corp was forcing all the other suckheads into drinking "vegan" processed blood; environmentalists who hated Crimson's obnoxious man-made mountain; and of course, smaller blood-manufacturing companies that Sullivan wanted to crush before they could become a threat.

I was surprised he hadn't thrown a few of his money-grubbing ex-wives on the list for good measure, because Lord knew he probably had plenty.

The whole list was crap, and I knew it just as well as the wolf did. My only concern was that Alathia might have been taking him seriously. That she couldn't see him for what he actually was: a snake oil salesmen, trying to get *us* to be the damn mongeese.

As far as I was concerned, Sullivan was at the top of my suspect list, lack of evidence be damned. As for Alathia, I had no idea what she was thinking ... and worse, I'm not sure I even cared. To be honest, I wasn't even sure if I could trust myself to share a backseat with her. Not without tearing into her. Literally.

I huffed and kept trudging down the path and off the trail, farther and deeper into the man-made forest.

I hated having these thoughts, but as I gazed up at the moon, I forgave myself. It was in its waxing gibbous phase, and just like in the Bronx, unfortunately, this side of the world was only 48 hours away from the next full moon. I needed to solve this case by then, so that I, and the wolf, could go into lockdown.

So I wouldn't hurt people.

Much as I didn't want her to, my wolf was taking over. She was getting hungrier, more restless, more bloodthirsty with each passing hour, and when she was like this even the most minor transgressions became reason for war. She needed to blow off some steam.

I groaned, dropped to one knee, and grabbed my head and shut my eyes tight, to keep the world from spinning. I was exhausted, needed sleep. But the wolf did not.

Let. Me. Out.

The lupine threat twisted around my mind, and against my will, my body began to listen. She had been quieter in the park earlier, but the coming moon and the crazy events of tonight had rattled her cage.

"Let me out, Samira." As the inhuman growl crawled out of my mouth, I slapped my hands over it, trying to silence it. But no, she kept talking.

If you'd just accept what you are, she taunted. *We would no longer be separate. We would be one. As we should be.*

I shook my head. "Being one with you means that humans will die."

Humans are born to die. They are supposed to die. But we, we are immortal.

"Stop."

Why? Because for you, being Arcane means being here forever with me? Her laughter echoed inside my thoughts. *Because it means being forever alone?*

"Be quiet ..." I snarled, and somehow my voice and hers had become intertwined. The change was coming upon me. "I'm warning you."

Such a shame. Purebreds like us do not have such qualms. Every single one of us accepts that we were born this way... everyone except you. No wonder your mother threw you into the trash—

"SHUT UP! JUST SHUT UP ALREADY!"

I will ... but only if you let me out.

I opened my eyes and laid my forehead on my knee, nearly giving in. Sweat beaded on my brow. Every month it was like this. Every month I hated it. I hated all of it, who I was. But it didn't mean the wolf wasn't right.

"I'll let you out," I said finally. "But you need to focus on this mission. You need to hunt. Hunt down that Lycana Benjamin Jama was with. *Hunt* ... not kill."

I won't kill any of our own. Not unless I have to.

"No humans, either!" I snapped.

Ugh ... if you insist. But in two days, they won't be so lucky.

"Whatever. Just stay focused."

You know what to do.

I did. I dropped my knee and closed my eyes again, forming a picture in my mind. The girl in my mind's eye loosened the leash, setting the wolf free. I watched the wolf grow, watched it fill the white space of my mind with its form. As it did, everything inside my body—bones included—liquefied, stretched, expanded, changed.

Those we bite—those humans who contracted our affliction through force—must break bones and rip skin to become what we were. But not natural-borns like me. We merely "shifted," and I—I was now clay beneath the fingers of a supernatural force.

My organic gel of flesh, platelets, DNA, and matter finally began to take its true form. My spine elongated and created a tail. My limbs re-solidified, physically inverted from their human form. My face length-ened, and so did my ears, which culminated in furry tips.

My entire body grew, and though I wasn't nearly as big or as imposing as I was during the full moon, I was massive enough for anyone to see that I was not the average-sized dog.

The clothes I wore ripped and fell away, including the phone that Aikan had given me. I whined and stumbled away from the phone, the human in me vaguely remembering that I needed to keep that connection open, just in case.

The human hairs on my skin sprouted into a thick, sleek coat of fur, fur that held the color of midnight, except for the diamond-shaped underbelly of auburn and gold. Long curved canines tore through top and bottom gums that had widened, darkened—and overcome by new instincts, I reared back my head and howled.

The wail tore through the night. The trees rustled. The wildlife scattered. And the wolf smiled as the heavens moved for her.

When the wolf opened her eyes, the world suddenly sharpened to the thousandth degree. She didn't care about Sullivan's list of suspects, and her anger toward Alla melted away. Most of my human thoughts disappeared into a dark compartment of the wolf's mind. The only thing she—*we* knew now was what was in our snout.

The smell of Jama's Lycan. The acrid smell of the rubber of his shoes, which marked out the many trails he'd walked on Crimson Corp's grounds. A trail that once led into one of Crimson Corp's idling cars. A car that had been here only three nights before and had left traces of its tires, exhaust, and the pheromones of two male occupants. One I didn't recognize, but it probably belonged to the driver.

The other was Jama's.

The wolf swished her tail, ready to go, but I stopped her. I turned to the phone and clothes that lay on the ground.

Bury it.

The wolf huffed, but she knew the human command was more than just a power move. It was about covering our tracks. Survival.

A few digs with my massive paw created a deep hole, and I dropped in my clothes and phone. I covered it and patted it flat. The cover-up wasn't exactly "good as new," but it'd be tough to see it in the dark. We'd be back long before dawn.

I turned toward the burns, and the male sweat, and the smells of furtive dealings in the air—shifted my nose toward the days' old trail Jama and his driver had left—and I took off. Once again, nature cowered before my form, moving out of the way as I tore through the world at supernatural speed.

My hunt had begun.

17

VAMPIRES AT THE PIANO BAR

ALATHIA

IN THE BACK of the Jaguar as it cruised from Crimson Corp toward Sandton, I was both irritated by and guilty for how things had gone with Samira in Damon Sullivan's office. She had arrived late to the meeting, which already put her on the back foot, and she looked a little—I don't know—spooked? At first, I thought she'd taked so long in the bathroom because she was primping, but when I saw how on edge she was when she joined us, it was obvious something else had happened. She had been jumpy and abrasive. She'd avoided eye contact with me. Had one of the guards assaulted her in some way? Or was it because it was so close to the full moon? Something was definitely up with her, and I had to find out what. But it would have to wait because first I would follow up on my best lead. Not searching for the doomsday prepper, nor checking the list of possible suspects that Sullivan had given us. I had something more interesting to investigate.

"I take it that Miss Shaw decided to make her own way home?" ventured Edgar, glancing at me in the rearview mirror.

"She likes to run," I said.

"At this time of night?" he asked.

"At this time of the month," I said, which promptly ended the conversation.

I didn't need to ask if he had organized the cleanup of our office. You never had to ask Edgar anything twice. Sometimes you didn't even have to ask him once; he just knew what you needed and got it done. Samira was right; the man was worth his weight in gold. Once we got the Crimson Corp payout, Edgar was in for a raise and a generous bonus.

Unable to focus on the case, my mind kept drifting back to Samira. I hadn't wanted to upset her, but we had no alternative but to take the job. Didn't she see that? I sighed loudly and sat back against the luxury suede. We'd be there in a few minutes, and I had to pull myself together.

Sandton was buzzing with lights and traffic and rat-racers eager for their slice of the "play hard" pie. They'd done the work, sweated in their suits, and now it was time to loosen their ties and let their hair down to burn the money they'd spent the day making. The drivers of luxury cars leaned on their horns, hooting next to bashed-up minibus taxis, phones rang, people yelled. Some would go straight from their open-plan offices to their favorite bars, others to open-air restaurants to eat sushi and oysters with Tabasco sauce and peri-peri prawns. Coffee shops, late-night shopping, luxury liquor-licensed cinemas. In Sandton, you don't need to look far for some place to spend your money. Humans in Johannesburg seem to have an insatiable need to move, move, move. Headlights and taillights, screeching tires, billboards the size of baseball fields. Gold shining, diamonds flashing, smart watches beeping. Walking, running, driving, working, spending, go, go, go.

I understood their motivation. They have short lives and feel the need to pack every interesting experience they can into the limited time they have, or they feel they've wasted it, wasted everything. It's what makes them scared of death … the fear that they haven't lived enough. Watching them makes me exhausted. Instead, I waited for the car to make the final turn, then reapplied my signature red lipstick.

The Jaguar glided to a halt outside the private members' club, and my door opened. I stepped out of the vehicle, my silver-tipped boots flashing on the red carpet of the spotlit entrance. Giving Edgar a wave, I made my way into the grand building.

The exclusive Magnate Club heritage building is a formal, elegant Edwardian style mansion which holds a rich history. Founded in 1886, in the fledgling days of Johannesburg, it has since been raided, visited by royalty, occupied by striking miners, and devastated by fire. They rebuilt, refurbished, and reasserted their position as a timeless South African icon, continuing to preserve the grandeur of a bygone era. They boasted a "diverse" group of members. The humans most likely thought this meant that they no longer discriminated on the grounds of gender, religion, or race. While that was true, what humans didn't realize was that the Magnate Club also didn't discriminate on the grounds of species. While the humans played snooker in the billiards room, drank brandy in the main bar, and danced in the ball-room, there was another rich cultural scene taking place parallel to their recreation. Just below their marble pillars and grand pressed tin ceilings were similar rooms: old oak-paneled libraries and green-carpeted cigar lounges. An armory room, and a balding red velvet curtained theater stage. A huge dining room where they held fancy full-moon feasts once a month. The humans didn't know about this mezzanine level, the button of which was hidden in the ancient copper elevator. What was also hidden from the natural folk were the supernatural beings who visited that floor. Vampires in the piano bar; witches in the coffee nook. The Arcane level was always buzzing with urbane city creatures having business meetings, consulting the sacred texts, or just getting their chill on.

Although urged to sign up as a member, I hadn't taken the bait. I still resented the fact that they hadn't allowed women to enter the building fifty years ago except as cleaners and cooks. Samira guffawed when I told her that, saying that South Africa was a completely different place a half-century before and that if I kept carrying that chip on my shoulder, it was going to get heavy. It's true; vampires hold grudges. You have to have a good memory if you plan on living for centuries.

I strode up to the concierge desk, a monumental slab of polished wood and metal. A human would probably be forgiven for thinking the woman standing behind it was a supermodel. She had clear, warm hazelnut skin, and she was wearing a beautifully cut suit, complete with a bow tie. A glinting gold pin on her jacket read, simply, "Molly." I was just about to warm to her when she hardened her face and spoke. A fake smile curled her lips but didn't reach her perfectly made-up eyes.

"Good evening," she said, showing me all her perfect white teeth. I felt a stab of envy. I have a thing about teeth.

"Good evening," I replied, laying my arm on the counter between us and looking deep into her eyes. "I'm here to meet a friend. Can you point me in the direction of the Maximilian Bar?"

"May I have your name?" she asked, manicured fingernails hovering above her keyboard. It was all a polite skit, of course. She knew I wasn't a member, and she had no intention of letting me in. I decided to play along.

"Du Pont," I said. "Esmeralda Du Pont."

The receptionist's fingers played over the keys. Her blank screen mirrored the expression on her face. "Your membership number isn't coming up."

I smiled. "I'm not a member. I'm meeting someone."

"Ah," she said, returning my tight smile. "I'm sorry. I'm afraid this is a members-only club."

When I glared at her, she added: "We don't make exceptions. Ever."

"That's not a problem," I said, pulling out my silver crocodile skin wallet. "I've been meaning to join for years." I took out my platinum credit card and held it out to her.

"It doesn't work like that," she said. On the counter between us, her fingers left water vapor prints that disappeared as soon as she lifted her hands. Ghost prints. She was feeling uneasy. I didn't blame her. There was a vampire wearing fabulous lipstick and designer boots trying to breach her line.

"Tell me how it works," I said, ignoring the urge to check my watch. It would have been much quicker to scale the back wall.

"There's an online application process," she said. "Then an interview. If you're accepted, you'll need to sign an agreement to abide by the club's rules and regulations."

It *definitely* would have been quicker to scale the back wall. I didn't have time for this muggle nonsense. I leaned in closer to the receptionist until all she could see and smell was me. I locked my gaze onto hers until I felt a psychic connection. and then I focused on it, an invisible rope of sparks joining our minds. She felt it too and stopped blinking. I had her full attention.

"Molly," I said, slowly and clearly. "I am Esmeralda Du Pont, and I am a member here. You will let me in, and once the elevator returns, you will forget that this ever happened."

She remained stone-eyed.

"Molly," I said. "Do you understand?"

After a long pause, she nodded and said: "Yes."

I marched over to the giant copper elevator and left her standing at the counter with her vacant stare. Just as I stepped over the threshold, she called out to me.

"Ms. Du Pont," she said, and I froze. Then I turned and looked over at her.

She showed me a slice of her perfect teeth. "Have a wonderful evening."

18

WOLFSBANE

SAMIRA

As I TROTTED up to the edge of a man-made garden, the wolf in me whined and instinctively lay down behind a hedge of rhododendrons. The night muted their usually splashy colors, but I sniffed them and shoved my muzzle through the foliage. On the other side of the brush, we could see a swanky little dive. It wasn't crappy enough to call "hole in the wall," but it was certainly nice enough for its owners to have planted two meaty bouncers firmly at its front door.

We'd either have to mow them down or avoid them in some way, because Jama's scent had led us right to this place.

My gaze caught the name of the club, glowing faintly above what was supposed to be a speakeasy door. The Wolfsbane. How original. Should have been called The Wolfsbush, if you asked me. Because that was all I could smell on this place: vagina. And lots of it. That honestly only meant one thing: Jama's Lycan date had been a Lycana prostitute.

Only one way to find out ...

Time to go. But when I urged the wolf forward, the argument started.

Not me, she complained. *It's your turn.*

I scoffed. Her range of emotions wasn't as complex as mine, but I felt a degree of awkwardness in her belly. "What do you mean *my* turn?" I whispered, and my tail swished again. "You're so badass, right? Then get your furry butt in there, and show them who's boss!"

But the wolf definitely did not "get her furry butt in there." Very much the contrary. Instead, she whined from the bushes, not knowing which made her feel more awkward: the fact that we'd tracked Jama's scent to a whorehouse, or that she couldn't get into said whorehouse unless she let the human take over again.

A human who would be stark naked, to boot. Because we had no clothes to put on. What to do?

A shadow fluttered on the side of the building, around the corner from the guards. My gaze shifted as it caught my attention, and for a moment, I thought—no, I *knew*—someone else was lurking around. The wolf growled. I might not have recognized him, but she did.

Holy cat scat. It was that doomsday prepper that Sullivan told us about. He was here.

I prowled around the perimeter of the garden, keeping as low as I could as I followed him. As a wolf, my body wasn't petite enough for full-on motion, so we crept, trying to get a better view of him.

Yep. It was definitely that prepper, and once again, he had his spray can, military gear, gun, and all.

Yeesh, did this guy have any concept of dressing for stealth, or did he stay ready for the apocalypse? Either way, I was looking at him, more interested in the T-shirt and pants that hugged his body than anything else.

I'd just found my change of clothes.

· · ·

I forced most of the wolf back in her cage; as I did, my body began to devolve and shrink back to human size. She didn't complain this time as she let the woman take the lead in both mind and muscle, and in the next moment, I was Samira again.

Naked.

Even though I was still warm from the transformation, that wouldn't last long. I needed to ambush this guy, snag his clothes, and then sneak in before someone spotted me with my tail in the air. Literally.

The only things separating me from him were the bushes and the 50 feet of parking lot I'd have to cross to get to him.

But how was I going to do that without him spotting me?

Watching and waiting, I crouched in the bushes. The prepper faced the back door of the club, moving his hands around, keeping them low and close to his body. *Ugh, please don't let him be jerking off—*

The sudden soft *click*, followed by a flash of light, disabused me of my assumptions. He was just taking pictures of the place. A perfect opportunity. I rose up on my haunches, ready to run and pounce. Even in my human form, I was still faster than most humans. He'd barely see me coming.

A mechanical whir hummed through the air. One that was quieter and wasn't coming from his camera. My ears pricked up, and my gaze followed. Immediately, I saw in the dark what he as a human could not: the hidden camera perched on the corner of the building. It'd just turned *right* toward him.

Someone was watching.

I tensed; I couldn't move until the camera did. Luckily, I didn't have to wait long.

The parking lot exploded with activity.

The back door slammed open, and at the same time, the two bouncers who'd been at the front of the club now flanked him on each side, charging him with guns drawn. They shouted and spat commands at him, and he dropped his phone as he put his hands in the air.

I saw the UV flash grenade in his hand before they did.

As the grenade dropped, I covered my eyes, and in the next second, the world behind my lids was set ablaze with white fire. It didn't hurt me as much as it annoyed me, but right now, it was blinding the hell out of those vamp guards.

Seizing my chance, I bolted out of the bushes toward the door, letting my nose and my ears guide me, trusting my skin to feel its way through the chilly night. I ran. The light was my cover; the guards' screams muted my stealthy, soundless dash through them all into the club.

No one saw me but him.

As I passed I felt his eyes on my body, hear the electronic hum of his night-vision goggles as we ran past each other. I, to the club, and he to his escape.

"What the ...?"

"Thanks, pal."

We muttered these to each other as we blazed by and yet neither of us stopped. He dashed into the night, and before the back door closed, I slipped inside the building. Both of us had made it, leaving cursing, blinded vamps in our wakes.

19

DEATHLESS HEART

ALATHIA

THAT SUPERMODEL RECEPTIONIST gave me a bad feeling. Watching her as the elevator doors slid closed, I shook my head to clear it of distracting thoughts. I needed to get the intel and get out of there. I cast my eyes toward the wall of engraved metal. If I had pressed any of the buttons one to three, I would have been going up to the regular floors, where magic was only a figment of their imagination. If I had removed the panel below that and selected the secret mezzanine level, I would have found the werewolves in the steak restaurant and the mermaids in the heated pool. But I wasn't after recreation. Instead, I pushed the very last button, which was still new and shiny, because no one ever went down there. My stomach sank along with the copper cube that was carrying me.

Loneliness enveloped me for a moment, traveling down into the earth alone. I thought of my argument with Samira and my break up with Frank. I alienated people; I knew I did. I refer to my heart as dead, because in a way it is. I mean, it beats along with the best of them, it pumps the blood that feeds my body, but I always imagine it as a small dead creature. A finch, perhaps. Cold, silent, stiff. Legs in the air. I'm supposed to be immortal—unless something *really* goes wrong, which is entirely possible, given my career—but sometimes I think that if my heart is going to keep living forever then is it really alive? Doesn't my heart's very deathlessness make it dead, in a way? I shook my head again, trying to clear it. It wasn't the time for such convoluted thoughts. What I was thinking didn't even make sense, not really. It was more of a feeling than a thought.

The elevator reached the end of the track, slowed, and shuddered to a stop. The doors slid open and I stepped out of the rich warm space and into the cool dank air of the lower basement.

"You're not allowed down here," came a voice out of the dark, startling me.

"I know," I said.

The elevator closed behind me and its gears ground, returning to the supermodel receptionist. There was no going back, and I couldn't step forward, either, because the darkness was a heavy shroud that kept me immobile.

"I'm calling security," the voice said, but he didn't move or pick up a phone.

Usually, I would mesmerize the people standing in my way of working a case, but I couldn't see the guy, never mind make intimate eye contact. I needed to find another way.

"I need your help," I said.

"You've got the wrong guy," he said.

"I beg to differ."

"I'm not one of those knights-in-shining-armor types."

"Good," I said. "Because I'm not one of those damsels-in-distress types."

It was weird having a conversation with the dark. In a way, it could have summed up my biology. And my entire social life.

"If you go back upstairs," he said. "I won't tell security you were here and you can leave in peace."

"I don't want to leave in peace," I said. "I told you, I need your help."

I heard him sigh. "You're one of those."

One of which? A detective? A vampire? A lonely woman with a death-less heart?

"'One of those?'" I said. "What is that supposed to mean?"

He sighed again. "You're one of those people who always get their way."

Oh. Well. Maybe I am. But it certainly wasn't always this way.

"Why are you standing in the dark?" I asked.

"I set up a tripwire in the elevator. If it comes down here, it trips the lights. It warns me of a possible intrusion and floods the place with darkness so that no one wants to enter."

"I want to enter," I said. Despite the dark.

"I thought you'd say that." There was resignation in his voice, and then I heard a clicking sound and the ceiling lights came on, one after the other in a row, like falling dominoes made of light.

"Ah," I said at he sight the man. He was wearing a stylish black hoodie and glasses with matching frames, which he pushed up the bridge of his nose in a gesture that reminded me of Clark Kent. He held a waxed-paper fair-trade coffee cup in his hand and his pants tapered at the bottom. Thousands upon thousands of books us, and there was a lone desk behind the hipster, on which sat a large computer, humming, and an empty chair.

"I still think you should turn around and leave," he said, pushing his specs up again, distracted. "If they find you down here, there'll be hell to pay."

"It's worth the risk," I said. "I have a murder weapon in my pocket."

20

THE ARCANE ASS FACTORY

SAMIRA

STILL NAKED AS A JAY, the darkness of The Wolfsbane dressing area covered me as I tiptoed through. Without even needing to traverse the whole building, all my senses gave me a multi-dimensional view of the place.

The club deserved more credit. What it lacked in appearance on the outside, it made up for with glamour within. From the bottom to the very top, the club was decked out.

On this floor, hundreds of feet away from me, stood a welcome desk. Oak, if my nose served me correctly. Stretching behind it was the foyer, piano bar, and gentlemen's club. Humans populated this entire floor.

Some of them were concierge staff. Others were servers and cigar girls. Many others were just pretty perfumed advertisements for the sensual delights that awaited.

Still, all that was just a cover.

I wrinkled my nose at the smell of synthetic fur shrugs that hung around the girls' tender necks. They wore plastic and polymeric fiber, not real fur, not real Lupine flesh. These human service girls were pretending to be *us*—Lycana—to give men a heightened experience.

But it was just a facade. If there was any recreation happening here that wasn't sex, this was the only floor where that was the case. The men with real money got to go upstairs, where they'd traipse through 12 floors of pure whorehouse and then tussle with the *real* wild animals. An Arcane ass factory if I ever smelled one.

On the roof, an indoor penthouse-sized lounge wrapped around an Olympic-sized saltwater pool. Even from here I smelled the brine and heard sylphs slinking playfully through its waters.

For about ten more floors beneath that, though, I smelled the themed sensuality—"winter wolf" on floor 11 and "mountain mane" on floor 10. Despite the personalized decor, all the levels shared the same purpose. The heavy smell of sweat and pheromones wafted through every mahogany crack and velvety surface of the boudoirs above. What my ears heard in tandem made me blush; it was a struggle for me to ignore the crude moans and heady pillow talk.

All of it sank down through the ceiling, weighing on my senses like a fog. The only humans here were men; the women, however? All Lycana. And I'd bet my entire fridgeful of franks that Jama's girl was here.

I continued my prowl through the club. My senses allowed me to avoid the roaming guards, and after a pair strolled past me, I finally found a dressing room and quietly slipped in. Thank goodness vampires preferred the dark. Otherwise, they'd have spotted my bare ass from a mile away, my senses be darned.

The dressing room was empty and quiet.

More than likely, all the girls were working upstairs. It didn't take long for me to sniff out some clean garments that were my size ... but as I flicked through the rack, I groaned in annoyance. There was nothing here but cosplay and role-play outfits, and *all* of them were some form of furry puppy fashion.

"Guess I have to ..."

I grabbed the one that would cover most of my bits and threw it on. It was a fur-lined, G-string monokini, and yet, it was still the most modest of all the outfits. Thank *God* Alathia wasn't here to see this. I turned to leave, and a slice of my body reflected from a mirror I hadn't noticed.

I took a minute to fix my hair. A wise choice, because there were twigs and flower petals sticking out of my voluminous 'fro. Not sexy. I styled myself and also arranged the remaining petals into something more festive. "Spring wolf" or whatever. Maybe someone would believe I was the new girl.

I looked at the mirror and took a huge breath, a little more nervous than I'd liked to admit. "Ok, Samira. Let's do this."

"Whatever *this* is had better be sucking or shagging, because I'm about to call my bosses about an intruder."

A voice behind me, one that belonged to someone I somehow hadn't smelled, spun me around. Two golden eyes cut through the dark in front of me, hovering above a chair wedged between two coat racks. My eyes immediately focused on the sexy slender outline of a woman sitting cross-legged, donned in a similar lack of garments.

But still, how did I not hear her? *Smell* her?

In the dark, she lifted a handheld device. A buzzer, probably. But she wasn't pressing down on it. She was hesitating. Waiting.

"Unless of course," she continued, "your visit is of some use to me, little omega. Is it? Or are you a waste of time?"

I straightened up, still shocked, but now poised for a potential fight. Her threat lingered in the air. "Let's make a trade."

"I'm listening."

"I'm looking for information."

"In exchange for what?"

I paused and thought. What did all wolves want most? For me, it was family. But for those who already *had* families ...

"Your freedom," I said finally. That was it. It was what we all wanted, whether alpha, omega, lone wolf, or pack hound. We all wanted, *needed*, the chance to roam. "I will give you your freedom."

21

THE X-BLADES

ALATHIA

I HAD the hipster librarian's attention.

He didn't look afraid; I wasn't threatening him. Instead, his eyes were alight and keenly focused.

"Show me," he said.

I lifted the pair of antique scissors out of my handbag. They were in a Ziploc bag, still painted with blood.

The man nodded his head almost imperceptibly and then gestured for me to join him at the large table in the center of the vast room. He retrieved a pair of latex gloves from a box on his desk and snapped them on, then sat down at the table on a small circular-seated wheeled chair and carefully extracted the weapon from its clear plastic pocket. He laid it carefully on the table, reached for a brush and some kind of solvent in a bottle, and set to work cleaning it. He worked quickly, efficiently, methodically. That kind of concentration says a lot about a man; I was mildly attracted to him.

That's when I saw the tattoo on the back of his neck. A pair of upside-down 3-D pyramids tilted toward one another, forming the letter "W."

"You're a wizard?" I asked.

He paused for a split second, then resumed working. "Yes."

"We don't get many wizards in this city."

"Yep," he said.

"You must get lonely down here," I said, then immediately regretted it. I had meant it as a genuine comment, but I worried that it sounded like a cheap come-on. I wanted to follow it up with "Don't worry, I'm not trying to seduce you," but I kept my mouth closed. It wasn't entirely truthful. I always liked to keep my options open, especially with good-looking hipster librarian wizards. The man saved me from my rambling internal monologue by replying.

"I don't get lonely," he said. "I have everything I need down here."

Taking in the hundreds of shelves, thousands of books, and neat boxes of mystery treasures, I saw his point.

"Can I take a look around?" I asked.

"No."

I liked him more by the second. I got another eyeful of the beautiful books, and when I looked down again, the scissors were shining brightly under the light of the desk lamp, and the wizard was polishing them with a soft cotton cloth.

"Look at this," he said, showing me the inside blade, hidden when the scissors were closed. There were three words engraved there: DE OPPRESSO LIBER.

"The oppressed will be liberated," he translated.

Of course, wizards understood Latin. He picked up his phone and started photographing the artifact from all angles, including a few shots with a silver ruler by its side. Then he reached for an oblong box roughly the same size as the scissors and placed them inside, cushioning them with bubble wrap.

"I assume you want this back," he said, handing me the sealed plastic bag with the bloody cotton and brush inside. "We don't have a DNA analysis machine here."

I took it and pushed it back into my bag, then put my hand out for the box containing the artifact, but the librarian didn't hand it over.

"Can I have them back?" I asked.

"No," he said and pushed his glasses up the bridge of his nose again.

I glared at him.

"These are the X-Blades," he said as if I should know what that meant. "They're extremely valuable from a historical point of view. They should be returned to who they were taken from. I know you have things to do, so I'll save you the trouble."

"What are you talking about?"

"The X-Blades were stolen a few weeks ago from the Magical History Museum in New York City. They were replaced by an excellent fake, but the curator noticed there was something amiss and had them inspected. Once the theft was confirmed, she sent a Hot Note to all the artifact guardians in the world. It's how I identified the object. I recognized it from the Note."

"You're an artifact guardian," I said. The man grew more attractive by the minute.

"Even if I wasn't," he said. "It would be the right thing to do."

I clenched my jaw. I guess he had a point. Besides, I already had what I had come for.

"Can I have your phone number?" the wizard asked.

The cheek of him. I narrowed my eyes tThe cheek of himhen realized he was holding his phone, ready to send the evidentiary photos he had taken. I gave him my number.

~

"I'll walk you out," the wizard said. The party was clearly over.

"Don't worry, I won't steal anything on the way."

"That's not why I'm accompanying you."

We waited at the elevator as it made its way down to us. The buzzing of my phone in my hand interrupted our uncomfortable silence. His message appeared on the screen. The contact name said "Vale".

I looked at him. "My name is Alathia."

He had a hint of a smile on his face. I could smell his warm skin, and it made me feel excessively hungry. Best to get Edgar to stop at the Crimson synth drive-through on the way home. I took a deep breath, then the elevator pinged and the doors slid open. I didn't trust myself alone with him in such an enclosed space.

"I can take it from here," I said, stepping in. "Thanks again."

"I insist," he said, stepping in after me.

I backed away from him, standing as far from his delicious scent as I could without appearing rude. He caught me gazing at his neck, and I quickly looked away, studying the old buttons of the elevator instead of his fang-zinging flesh.

"I was wondering—" he said, but before he could finish his sentence, the lift chimed and the doors slid open, and all hell broke loose.

A crowd of bustling people in the entrance hall of the Magnate Club all turned to look at me. Uniforms, guns, flashing cameras.

"That's her," said the receptionist, pointing. The cops swarmed toward me, journalists on their heels. Before I could reach for the elevator button, Vale was there, pounding it, and the doors closed just a second before the uniformed police officers reached us. At a squeezing sensation, I looked down and saw it was Vale's hand wrapped around my upper arm.

"That didn't go as planned." I felt breathless.

"There's another way out," said the wizard. "I'll show you."

My mouth was dry, my thoughts raced. I had mesmerized the receptionist. How could she have remembered my face? They must have had a security team watching the cameras, and when the woman let a non-member into the club without remembering what had happened, someone pressed the panic button. But how did the press get there so fast? Perhaps they had been listening in to the cops' vehicle transmissions. This wouldn't do. I couldn't risk exposing the Masquerade. I had to be more careful.

Vale had selected the supernatural floor. As soon as the doors opened, we dashed out and down the emerald-colored passage. We sprinted past three large rooms—cigar smoke, chlorine, flame-grilled steak—and then turned the corner. Vale pushed me through a doorway and then slammed the door behind us.

"*Obfirmo,*" he muttered, and the lock clicked closed. There was the smell of sparks in the air; the after-scent of a spell. We were in the emergency stairwell, standing so close to each other, breathing one another's air.

"You okay?" he asked. I nodded. We raced down the stairs. On the other side of the next door was a dark parking basement. Vale passed me something round and cold. A helmet. Then suddenly there was a roar of a motorbike and there he was, revving, waiting for me to jump on. I blurred toward him and straddled the humming engine, the wizard's body up against my own. My anxiety was fading, taken over by a warm rushing in my pelvis. No longer afraid the police or the reporters would discovere me, I moved my hips closer to Vale's and held on while he accelerated out of the dark and onto the wet black streets.

22

THE BANE'S BOTTOM BITCH

SAMIRA

A DARK and silky chuckle twisted around the room, and immediately I knew that I said the wrong thing. "A wolf's freedom cannot be given. And it certainly cannot be given by the likes of you."

"I'm here to help."

"What do I look like, taking 'help' from an omega?"

"I'm not the one selling furry tacos and giving humans hand jobs so that I can make a living."

The insult cut into her. I watched her eyes narrow. The alpha pride. A weakness that most leading werewolves shared. I pressed on, pulling what little rank I could.

"Maybe I haven't been around the block as many times as you ... but I've never met an alpha who couldn't feed or protect her pack. Have you?"

"You don't know a lick about me, *volchonok*. Keep talking trash, and I'll tear the black right off your face. It might actually make you look better."

I snorted. One would've thought that us being werewolves would, maybe, outweigh the race issues, but they didn't. Truth was that we were only forced into wolf form once a month. The rest of the time, well, we walked the world as humans, didn't we? And while in the human world, this bitch had clearly drunk the supremacist Kool-Aid about her station versus mine.

Still, I ignored the insult, focusing instead on her body language as she rose from her chair smoothly, as would a goddess from a lake. Her eyes glinted in the dark, and she walked toward me. I should say "glided" toward me, because she'd mastered the art of the sashay. A lupine who had conquered the feline's gait. Apparently, she'd been a working girl a long time, because she wasn't even trying, really, and it made me just a little jealous. She didn't look as though she would attack, but she was closing the distance, and not in a congenial manner.

Ignoring her attempts to intimidate, I tensed and pushed on. "I'm Samira Shaw," I said. "I work for David Sullivan, President of Crimson Corp. *Privately*."

My throat clamped shut as I said this; I still didn't like that Sullivan dude, but technically I *was* working for him, and right now, that fact was helping me to *not* get pounded into a grease stain. The Lycan stopped short and stared at me with narrowed eyes. Something about what I said had gotten her attention.

"I am looking for a Lycan," I continued. "She was a friend of mine and Benjamin Jama's. He died a few hours ago. I ... I just thought she should know. "

The Lycan cut her gaze at me, sizing me up as I stood there. "For a lone runt, you have many 'friends.' Unusual."

I forced a smile. "Guess I'm a lucky girl."

"Given what's about to come for you, I certainly hope so." She lifted the remote. Shit. She'd already pressed the buzzer. From its head, a flashing red light blinked a signal. I didn't have much time.

"If your 'friend' Mr. Jama ever came here, he was no friend of any Lycana. Trust me. The men who come here aren't interested in friendship. And my instincts say that you aren't either. Why are you really here?"

"You ask that *after* you set the guards on me?"

She smirked. "I've only called the pit boss for my floor. And you've got about 30 seconds before he comes barreling through that door to tear your nosy little head off."

Oh great. I stole a glance at the door, and in the distance I heard the surprisingly rapid footfalls of something very heavy and *very* angry.

"I don't know who you are and what you really want," she continued. "But I honestly don't care. If you're serious about 'freeing your fellow lupines,' though, I'm all ears ... but of course, I'll need to see a bit of what you can do first. If you can get through my pit boss, the other bosses upstairs, and help all of us walk out of here *alive*, then I imagine you might have something worthwhile to offer. And if so, I'll give you what you seek."

The footsteps were getting closer. I had 15 seconds, max. "When you say 'go through' your bosses—?"

"You're a werewolf. There's only one way we 'go through' anything. Don't be naive."

Fine. I squared my shoulders. "Jama was murdered and dumped into my office. I'm here to find out who might know more about it. I smelled a Lycan on him, and it seems she's a fan of, er... primrose feminine products."

Getting that last part out was awkward. Talking about what a Lycan used to keep her lady bits aired out between clients was one of the last things I wanted to do, but as this one had said, I only had 30 seconds.

"Hm. There are only a few girls here who even like that scent ... but oh, darn, here comes my bodyguard!" Her lips curled into a smile, and I turned to the door just as it slammed open.

A bouncer as big as a minivan somehow squeezed his way through the door. The darkness on his face could've eclipsed an entire moon, and beneath it was muted violence. He took a step forward, and I tensed, ready to fight.

Then the girl in me overrode the wolf, and she gave me a mental command that made total sense.

"Wait!" I shouted, holding up my hands. "I'm not here to cause trouble, sir. I'm just here looking for work."

The bouncer hesitated. He didn't look convinced, but he was listening.

"I'm really sorry I snuck in," I admitted, and I forced a girly shame onto my face. I added a pout for good measure. "I'm just looking for work, and ... I didn't know of any other way in except to, you know, audition?" And I motioned to my role-play outfit sheepishly. I was brand new and all thumbs with this whore-for-hire thing, and because it was true, I pulled it off. The veil of suspicion on his face lifted, but only by half.

Narrowing his eyes, he looked to the long-limbed Lycan next to me. "*Eto pravda?*" He demanded.

I cast a nervous glance at the Lycana. Would she blow my cover? She looked at me and smirked. Then she tossed her hair back and lifted her chin.

"*Da,*" she said smoothly. "I was helping her get dressed and giving her some pointers before I called you. She wants to see the big bosses. To earn big money. Not many around here that look like her, *prava?*"

The bouncer relaxed. Whoever this Lycana was, she seemed to have some pull around here.

"Fine," he breathed out finally. A heavy Russian accent infused his words. "You. Come." And he snatched me by the upper arm and dragged me out like a ragdoll.

"Toodles, *kotik*," the Lycan snickered. "If you make it back from your meeting with that 'gift' you promised me, I'll be here waiting. We *all* will."

The Lycan's cold sneer followed me out and ran an invisible icy finger down my neck. To anyone else it just sounded like cute girl talk, but to me? It sounded like the 'Bane's bottom bitch and I have just struck a deal.

23

MAKE VAMPIRES GREAT AGAIN

ALATHIA

WE ZOOMED out of the Magnate Club basement and down the street, dodging luxury sedans and zipping by tuk-tuks. I clung on to Vale's waist, enjoying the sensation of the bike thrumming below me and the feel of his body against mine. We rode six blocks north and then turned in the direction of the city center. I saw my Jaguar gleaming under the sign of the Crimson Deli drive-through. I gestured to it and Vale got the message, slowed down and swung into the parking lot. While Edgar waited to pay for his order, I climbed off the bike and handed the helmet back to Vale. He locked it in his box and nodded.

"Thank you," I said.

"No bother."

"Well," I said. "That's not true. You didn't need to help me. And you'll probably lose your job now."

It was a real shame. It looked like a pretty cushy job for a wizard. I felt bad.

"No way," he said, pushing his glasses into place. "I was protecting an asset. The director of the Museum of Magical History will be very pleased. She'll make sure I keep my job at the Club."

"Oh, good," I said, relief allowing my shoulders to sag. It had been a long night. We looked at each other, and it was a moment of mutual affection. "Well, wizard," I said. "I guess I'll be seeing you around."

"Will you?" he said. "Are you planning on finding more stolen artifacts you'll need identified?"

"You never know," I said, and smiled at him. Then I turned and walked away, and as I reached the Jaguar, I heard his motorbike roar off behind me.

"Good evening, Miss Laurent," said Edgar as I climbed in and shut the door. "I took the liberty of ordering you dinner. I wasn't sure if you had eaten today." He passed me the red takeaway cup that non-magical people might think was a Cinnacola.

"Oh, Edgar," I said to him, taking the drink and settling back into my seat. "*Hvala Vam.* What would I do without you?"

My driver didn't speak Croatian, but he had learned a few key phrases over the years, like *Hvala Vam* (thank you); *zdravo* (hello) and *voziti!* (drive). At least, I thought that's what they meant. My Croatian was decades old and fairly rusty. I still knew how to swear, though.

The synthetic blood was the perfect temperature, salted, and infused with rosemary. It was my favorite flavor. I settled in and retrieved the list that Damon Sullivan had printed out for Samira and me from my pocket: people and organizations who wanted Crimson to fold. Top of the list was the Doomsday prepper, who I would go after the next day. Second was the Westcliff Residents Association, who were suing Crimson for building such a "revolting, brutalistic eyesore" in the heart of a usually beautifully treed suburb. The man-made mountain and emerald-glass cloudscraper had been contested since the day Sullivan had bought the land. The residents association had fought him tooth and nail since construction had begun, but word on the street was that Sullivan had greased so many palms that no one dared stand in his way.

Third on the list was the primordial Vampire Kinship, a coven of vampires older than the city. They were conservative Arcanes who held on to ancient vamp habits: wearing capes, sleeping in coffins, staying away from garlic, and avoiding sunlight at all costs, even though contemporary science had proven that neither UV rays nor any plant in the allium family had any negative effect on our species. The VK was not to be dissuaded by something as modern as "science" and believed the "Vegan Vampire" movement that Crimson Corp had enabled—buying blood in straws and takeaway cups instead of hunting for it—was a disgrace to our species. They called on younger vampires to revert to the old, "wholesome" ways. I guess they wanted to Make Vampires Great Again.

Then there was Red Kite. Red Kite was a small independent business which competed in the synthetic blood industry. They were forever taking Crimson to court for monopolizing the industry, price fixing, and other anti-competitive issues. A woman with an apparently unas-sailable code of ethics ran it, a corporate warrior who used the compa-ny's profits for good and did everything she could to "fight evil." Was Crimson Corp evil? Samira seemed to think so. If the owner of Red Kite thought so too, I wondered how far she would go to take them down.

The car slowed to a stop just as I'd finished skimming the list. I crum-pled the paper up and forced it into my empty cup, ready to throw into the recycling bins on the corner of my block.

My door swung open. "Would you like me to walk you up, Miss Laurent?"

I remembered that the killer had broken into our office, and for all intents and purposes, he may have done the same thing to my place.

But I was fit and strong, and I had my trusty old revolver strapped to my thigh, so I thought I'd be okay.

"No thank you, Edgar. I'll see you tomorrow."

"Yes, ma'am," he said, and tipped his hat.

I pushed through the main entrance doors and blurred up the stairs, using my thumbprint to open my apartment door. It was dark and empty, but something was off.

The place was empty now, but someone had been there. I smelled him. An unfamiliar man. Human. I stopped abruptly and sniffed the air; definitely a stranger. I wished at that moment that I had Samira's sense of smell. I'd be able to track the creep down. I flicked the lights on and saw a scribbled note on the hardwood floor of my entrance hall.

I felt a rush of relief. He hadn't broken in. He had slipped the piece of paper under the door.

"Alathia Laurent," the terrible handwriting read. "I'm a journalist. I saw you at the Magnate Club tonight. I know about the Arcanes and that you have the stolen X-Blades. I will report you to the police and blow the Masquerade wide open if you don't meet with me tomorrow. We have a mutual enemy we need to discuss. Don't be afraid. I mean you no harm." A scribbled line gave contact details. "I'll be waiting for your call."

24

BITCHES & TRICKS

SAMIRA

THE BOUNCER DIDN'T SAY a word to me, but it didn't take long for us to get into the elevator and ascend to the top floor. I snarled and tried to yank my arm away, but then I felt the muzzle of a revolver in my side.

It burned.

Silver bullets had been shot through it recently, and the silver-laced gunpowder residue, while slight, now burned into my side. When I stopped struggling, the bouncer removed the pistol, his message clear: I wasn't going anywhere. Not unless I wanted to be turned into a werewolf throw rug.

He shoved me through the halls of the top floor, and as I stumbled through the red-tinged corridor, I passed full-length glass windows. Through them, I now saw what I could only previously smell.

Lycans, servicing their clients. I tried my best to keep my eyes forward and off the various contortions of flesh behind the screens. But I'd already seen too much. Lycana, in various stages of transformation, being taken advantage of. Some were Lycanje too, for the men who preferred to walk on the other side.

Worse though, were the remnants of "experience" I saw in many of the empty cells. These were much bigger, and much more "dungeon-ish," complete with stone walls, thick Plexiglas, and retractable chains and manacles, made of iron so thick it could have moored a small ship. Massive iron muzzles hung on the walls as well.

Scattered across the stone floors were clumps of fur, and in some cells, dried blood was splashed across the walls.

Were some clients sexing Lycana *while* they were full-on werewolf? By *force?*

My stomach turned completely upside down, unable to handle both the disgust and the rage that filled me. These rapist, bestiality-loving mofos were definitely going to get a piece of my mind, and with any luck, I'd tear out a piece of theirs too.

The bouncer behind me grabbed my shoulder with a monstrous grip and when he pushed me again, it was into the office at the end of the hall.

"*Novaya shlyukha,*" he announced as he shoved me in. He closed the door behind him and locked it. "*U neye net vstrechi.*"

He directed this to the three other men who sat in the room, counting money. When they looked up, I got a mix of reactions. Strangely, none of them were surprised. He shoved me forward into the middle of the room.

"*Potomu chto ona zloumyshlennik.*" One of the vamps sneered, but then he eyed me—my body—with interest. "*Ochen' krasivyy zloumyshlennik.*"

I literally only knew about five words of Croatian from Alathia, and none of them were helping me. In fact, I think this was Russian.

The main one finally addressed me directly. "*Ty ishchesh' rabotu, kotenok?*" He swayed to a stand, his gaze pouring into mine. By the shit-eating grin on his face, kicking me out was *not* the thing on his mind.

"I don't know what any of that means," I snapped. "But it sounds like Asshole."

Chuckles rolled around the room, and smirking, the vampire addressed me again. "I asked you if you were looking for work, baby. Because if you are, we have openings. You'll have to give a good audition though. In fact, we have a fresh casting couch ready just for you."

I forced the growl back, but inside, the wolf nosed her way out of her cage. The Lycan had said to go "through" them; I didn't like the idea, but the more he taunted me, the more his death appealed to me. To the wolf.

"I like a bitch that does tricks. Do you do tricks, baby? Sit, stay, roll over ... fetch?"

The wolf leaped, and so did I, my body changing in mid-air.

"HOLY SHIT, SHE'S A SHIFTER!"

It was all the vamp could get out before I felled him and bit down into his throat. I closed my teeth on his flesh, tasted the sharp sting of the tannins of human blood, blood that he was *not* supposed to be consuming—then I snapped back, spraying it across the mahogany wall.

"DIMI! YOU FUCKING *BITCH*!"

Under the angry shout, I heard holsters unclip, the metal scraping against leather, but I was already leaping onto the next vamp, taking him out. I jumped to the wall, running along it and around it. The thunder split the air in two, and splinters chased my heels as bullets tore into the walls behind me. I pushed off the wall and leaped onto the next vamp.

The last bullet in his clip grazed me, burning a clean line through the obsidian of my fur. In the next second, he was swimming in blood. I lifted my head to the bouncer and licked my jaws.

His gun was empty, and his eyes were full. Of fear.

I advanced, snarling. "Don't move."

His hand reached for something in the waistband of his jeans, something hidden under the folds of his back fat.

"I said, *don't—*"

But he'd already pulled it. Before he could aim, I was on him, knocking him to the ground. He was stronger than the others, though, and used both arms to keep me at bay. I snapped my jaws at his neck viciously as he pushed me up and away. I swiped at his face with long steely claws. He screamed as his flesh was raked away.

I opened my jaws wide and slammed them closed on his arm. A satisfying *crunch* filled my mouth, blood gushing from the open wound of his now-broken arm. He screamed, and I growled and tore at him, at the flesh already ripped open.

I didn't notice the new gun until too late.

A bullet tore into my shoulder. I tried to crab back, my teeth entangled in the mess of flesh, skin, and leather. But as the gun muzzle lined up with my snout, I dodged and clamped down on the exposed sweaty, fleshy neck.

I bit so hard that my teeth met inside the bouncer's neck. He died instantly and so did the struggle in his limbs.

I whined, loudly, until it turned into a long howl, twisted with suffering. The burn in my shoulder was unbearable, and beginning to spread. As I stumbled back, my bones withered inside my limbs, my blood beginning to boil.

My transformation didn't last, and I was suddenly naked again. But this time, my shift back into human form was unnatural, sickening: the hair on my body fell off, almost in a uniform sheet, and with the coat gone I saw the acidic lesions spreading across my skin. Blood sweated through my pores as the silver ate away at me.

In the next few minutes, I'd be dead. The road to hell was going to be painful, and I hadn't even said goodbye to Alla.

The door to the office burst open, and I caught a blurry glimpse of who was there. It was the Lycan, the bottom bitch. Her jaw was open, her eyes wild and searching.

"See?" I whispered weakly. "Told you I could do it."

My legs crumpled, no longer able to hold up my weight. And as her face popped into view above mine, the world fell away, and the blackness in my mind swallowed me whole.

25

MONSTERS & MAGIC

ALATHIA

A HEADACHE and a mouth as dry as Mars woke me. It had been a night of tossing and turning. My anxiety about the ambitious journalist stalker had crept in and colored my dreams. I tried to call Samira again, but she was still not answering her phone. Where the hell was she? I had things to tell her, but mostly, I needed to know if she was okay. Guilt and worry embroidered my insides, sewing my stomach with black thread.

I had things to tell her. Like, Jama's killer had recently been to New York. And that we had a rogue reporter on our hands, threatening to cut the cookie dough. I needed her to sniff the note so we could find him and pounce, unannounced, and I could mesmerize the Masquerade out of him, *Men in Black* style, before it was too late.

I lay on my back, naked apart from a thin cotton nightie, my white linen sheets twisted at my feet. I stared at the ceiling, drumming my fingers on my stomach, figuring out what I would do next.

Damon Sullivan wanted us to investigate the doomsday prepper as the lead suspect. I wasn't sold. Sure, he looked like he was on the dark edge of crazy, but hanging around the Crimson Corp building with a backpack full of spray paint cans did not necessarily equate to being a sadistic killer. Plus, the X-Blades were stolen from the MMH in New York, and the prepper wasn't allowed to travel because of the pending cases against him. A loner like him ... I doubted he would have the money or contacts to get someone to steal them for him and then smuggle them to South Africa. The most puzzling thing for me was that he was a human. He shouldn't know anything about what Crimson Corp was doing. This is why paranoid delusionists scare me. Sometimes they don't know how close they are to the truth.

How much did the doomsday prepper know?

I could work my way down the list that Damon gave me, but something niggled at me, like a puppy chasing the hem of a skirt. The more I thought about it, the more I suspected the list was bogus. They all had motives to harm Crimson Corp, but I couldn't imagine the head of a residents association stealing a magical pair of scissors and pinning a man to the wall with them. No, I needed to dig deeper than that. I needed to find out who Jama was—who he *really* was—and why someone wanted him dead. Sullivan wouldn't let us search his office, but there were other ways to get to know a man.

I messaged Edgar to pick me up in half an hour, then showered, dressed, and scarfed down a couple of straws of chai-flavored blood. Forty-five minutes later ,I was outside Benedict Jama's house, my finger on the doorbell.

A young girl answered. She stood behind the black palisade gate, hands on the bars as if it were a prison cell door. She must have been eight or nine years old. She had long dark hair and a pale face tinged with pain. She reminded me a little of Wednesday from the Addams Family, but more than anything she reminded me of myself, when I was a child. I tried to not stare at her, but I felt an instant connection.

Usually I'm not a fan of children—especially of the human variety—but this girl made my heart contract.

"Hello," I said, trying my best to Not Act Creepy. "I'm here to see your mother."

She took her small hands away from the bars and bunched them up inside the pockets of her dark brown dress. "She's not seeing anyone today. She's not well."

There it was again, that twinge in my chest. "Of course. I understand."

The child turned to walk back into the house. The garden was pretty; prettier than you'd guess from observing the harsh-looking security wall topped with spikes.

"May I," I said, "perhaps speak to you? Ask you some questions?"

She gave me the side-eye. "I'm not supposed to talk to strangers."

"I'm not a stranger. Not really. Your dad's boss hired me to help find out what happened to him."

She looked at me with renewed interest, her hazel eyes glinting green in the morning light.

"I'm just trying to find out who hurt your family," I said. "So that he can be punished."

She didn't look convinced.

"I need your help to find him so that he can never do this to anyone else."

Conflicted, her small hands clenched and unclenched in her pockets. She knew she wasn't allowed to answer my questions, but her need to know what happened to her father was more urgent.

"Okay," she whispered, looking at her bare feet, her dark hair falling in her face. She brought out a small silver key and opened the gate, and I followed her down the neatly trimmed path toward the house. There were irises and lilies, and a trellis with climbing pink tea roses.

"This is a good garden for fairies," I said.

The girl turned and looked at me, then kept walking. "I don't believe in magic."

~

We settled in the lounge, which was homey and nicely decorated, if a bit worn. I found the contrast of the scruffiness of some of the furniture at odds with the very expensive suit that Benedict was wearing the day he died.

"My name's Alathia," I said. "My friends call me Alla."

Truthfully, I should have said my *friend* calls me Alla. I only had one. But she didn't need to know my problems. She didn't need more bleakness in her life.

"I'm Veronica," she said. "My dad used to call me Ron."

She looked at me with wide eyes, and I could see the rawness of her grief. I felt another contraction in my chest, as if someone was squeezing my heart with icy fingers. I stood up and turned away from her, sweeping my hair away from my face and craving more air to breathe. I needed to stand on top of a mountain far away from smoking golden cities and dead fathers. I needed to be in the clouds where it was just blue sky and oxygen. This room was too small for the magnitude of emotion we were both feeling.

Would I have come if I had known that Benedict Jama had a daughter? Maybe. But she had caught me off-guard with her Wednesday looks and her big sorrowful eyes. It was a mirror I didn't want to look into.

"Are you okay?" the child asked.

I tried to compose myself, wrapping my arms around my torso. I turned back to face her.

"What do you think happened to your father?" I asked. The stone in my throat made my voice gruff.

"I don't know," she said. "Mom said a Bad Man killed him."

"A Bad Man?"

"You know. Like the bogeyman that hides under beds."

"Yes."

"Maybe he was hiding under Dad's bed but Dad couldn't see him because he didn't believe in monsters."

"Do you believe in monsters?" I asked.

"Of course I do. Don't you?"

I nodded. "I do."

God knows I have seen enough of them in my line of work. Monsters and magic.

I cleared my throat, trying to dislodge the ache there. "Do you know anything about the Bad Man who killed your father?"

Veronica shook her head. "No. But Dad knew he was going to die."

I shot her a puzzled look. "Why do you say that?"

"He came into my bedroom a few days before he went missing and hugged me too tight. Told me that he'd always love me, even if he weren't around anymore. I thought he meant he had to spend more time at work—he was always at work—but after Mom told me what happened, I realized he knew that the Bad Man would get him."

So Benedict had known he was in trouble. His murder had been premeditated.

My voice was tender. "Is there anything else you can tell me?"

"I don't know anything else," she said, and I nodded. "Except that—"

She hesitated.

"Yes?"

"Except that maybe the Bad Man was a woman."

At a crashing sound then, I looked up and a woman barreled toward me, a bitter snarl on her face and a butcher knife in her hands. My hands shot up automatically, showing surrender, while also readying myself to fight if I had to. She stopped only a couple of feet away from me.

"Get out!" she shouted.

"Mrs. Jama," I said. "I apologize. I didn't mean to—"

"Get out of my house right now or I'll—" she made a stabbing motion at me, but didn't finish her sentence. I got the message.

"I'm leaving," I said.

"You should never have come!" There was a wild spark of madness in her eyes, and the dark curls on her forehead were wet with perspiration.

My hands were still in the air. "I'm here to help," I said. "I'm a detective."

The woman spat at my feet. "Get out!"

I looked at the young girl. "Veronica ..."

The mother growled then, like a dog. "Don't you dare speak to my daughter!"

"Veronica. I will find the person who did this to your family."

The girl nodded, blinking, trying to hold back her tears. I didn't want to leave her alone with her crazy mother, but it didn't look like I had a choice. Veronica ran past us and outside, fumbling for her key to open the gate for me.

What could I say to the woman?

That when I was a child, I had also lost my father to a Bad Man.

That I knew how that kind of violence ripped families apart.

That I would do *everything* I could to find out who did this to them.

26

THE OTHER WEREWOMAN

SAMIRA

THE FIRST THOUGHT in my mind when I woke up in bed wasn't a thought at all, but a big fat pile of goo. A stupid, wet smorgasbord of memory that wouldn't work for diddly-squat.

Lewd cackling, the wolf leaping, shots firing, blood spraying ... slivers of experience flickered in my mind, capped off by the sharp burn in my blood. That was all I could remember.

My body, on the other hand, seemed to remember every detail; it complained, slicked down flat with a fine sheet of agony. Felt like I'd been dumped in acid.

I took a deep breath and blinked. The room around me was dark, and my senses had been dulled almost to human level. Courtesy of the silver that jerk had shot me with. The blip of a heart monitor sounded on my right.

"You made it," a soft whisper threaded through the darkness. "For a while there, I wasn't sure you would."

I couldn't see the speaker, and when I tried to sit up, my world spun.

"Take it easy, okay?" The same voice again. "You're still on dialysis."

Dialysis?

I flexed my hands, conscious of the IVs threading into my veins. On *both* arms. Whatever they were pumping into me, they were doing it hardcore. I felt the cool creep of fluids through my limbs.

"Thank you," I murmured back finally. "Whoever you are."

"I'm the girl you've been looking for, Mr. Jama's 'friend.'"

That grabbed my attention, and despite the fact that I felt plastered, I tried to sit up again. I still couldn't see. She was too far away, probably on purpose, and with my senses practically hammered, there was no way I'd be able to ID her.

"I need to see your face," I said. "Please."

"That would be unwise, considering we clearly have a murderer on the loose."

"But I'm not him."

"Who said it was a 'him'?"

I swallowed hard. Partially from the dryness in my throat, and partly from embarrassment. She was right, of course. For all I knew, *she* could have put that body in our office.

"Whoever it is," I said again. "I need to find him. And I need your help."

"I have already helped you." Across the room, I heard the speaker get up to leave.

"Jama's murderer was after something. Maybe he wanted to expose someone or something. Maybe he killed him for sport," I breathed hard. Even talking was an effort. "I wonder who, or what, he'll hunt next now that his last victim's gone cold?"

The footsteps stopped at the door.

I pushed on. "If he *is* hunting... you *will* be next."

Silence in the distance. And then: "Even if that were true, miss, what can *you* do about it?"

I took another breath, struggling. "You ... clearly didn't see what I did to your bosses' office. Yet here you stand, enjoying the spoils of my labor, right?"

She said nothing. I sat up straighter in the dark, trying to focus on where I thought she was standing.

"I gave you your freedom," I pleaded. "Now please ... give me the truth."

After a moment, a light popped on right next to me. A soft blue from a nearby lamp. When my eyes finally adjusted, the Lycan sat at my bedside. A young, pretty little thing with large eyes and a glossy bob that touched her copper shoulders.

"I ... changed the bulbs for you," she explained with a sheepish smile. "It's a special moonlight bulb for, you know, *us*. Tricks the brain into thinking the moon is out. It's better for healing."

She was right. Whether the bulb was actually working or not, I felt stronger already. For the first time since I'd been shot, the wolf within stirred.

"You can change. *Shift*." She indicated my body, still broken but healing fast. "When we got to the office, I couldn't believe my eyes. The full moon's not for another day and a half, and still, you—how can you do that?"

I smiled. "Guess there are some advantages to being a runt, huh?"

She giggled. "Yeah, trying telling Alinka that."

I blinked and cocked my head. "Alinka?"

"Tall? Mean? Super competitive alpha bitch?"

Oh. Her. Well, good to know Miss Queen Sucks-a-Lot of Broad Mountain had a name.

"She didn't even want to bring you here. Said we should just leave, you know, before the authorities came. But I didn't think that was fair."

I smiled. Such a sweet girl. "Thank you, Miss ...?"

"Lila."

"Lila. Do you ... do this often?" I indicated the medical room around me. "Healing, I mean?"

"Only when a client wrecks a Lycana really bad. We rarely need to come here, but when we do—"

"Has Benjamin Jama ever sent anyone here?"

The question was abrupt, and it slapped her. But she answered anyway. "Oh no. Never. He was always a stressed man, but a gentle one. Not a single drop of violence in him. At least not toward me."

"So you used to see him."

"Yes. Quite often."

"And while he was here, did he *only* see you?"

"Not at first. At first, he did what most clients do and shopped around, to find one he liked. You know ... a favorite."

"And he chose you."

"I admit, I was surprised too. I'm so ... well." A blush spread over her cheeks. "I was 'inexperienced,' if you know what I mean."

Ah. So she'd been a virgin when they'd met. Jama liked his girls "innocent." Hmph. Men who wanted to take advantage of women and keep them quiet usually did. It made sense that he'd chosen her to be the other werewoman.

"I see," I said, betraying none of my cynical thoughts. "And how was your relationship with him after he 'chose' you?"

"Nice. Very nice. He was very kind to me. Said he loved me. And our child."

My eyes widened. Holy freakin' gonzola cheese. Jama had a love child on the side?!

"I know what you're thinking," she said quickly. "And, no, he didn't abandon us, not at all. He has a wife and daughter, and I understood that. He could have asked me to abort, but he didn't. He said it was my choice, and whatever I did, he would be there for me, for us, and he *was*. I want for nothing."

"So why are you still a prostitute?"

"Because that's one thing Benny couldn't do: buy my freedom. He really tried. He *did*, I swear it. He asked the vamps bunches of times, and they always said no. Said he made them more money as a client, and I as a whore. Said I would be working for them for a long time. For *forever*."

"In the days before his death, was he acting strangely?"

"Oh, yes. Stranger than ever before. Just four days ago, he came in crying, but he wouldn't tell me what was wrong. Said he'd done something good... but also very bad. For him, for his family, and for me. That he had just put us all in danger, and that we needed to get away. He gave me some money, set up all these untraceable accounts, and told me to run as far away from Johannesburg as possible. Told me to leave my pack, become a lone wolf. Told me to take our child far away."

"And he never told you why he was on the run?"

"No. Benny said if he told me anything, I could be killed. Said he loved me, and that he just wanted me to get away."

I sat back and set my jaw. Dark thoughts crawled through my mind. So Jama had been on the run, and I'd bet every hair on my tail that he'd been running from Crimson Corp. I'd have to check his work logs to confirm it, but if he'd been pulling long hours and then suddenly got spooked, maybe he'd seen something he shouldn't have.

"And he told you not even a single detail?"

She shook her head, upset. "No. But I think I know why he was so worried. Because I *saw* her once, across the street from The Wolfsbane. I ... I think she knows. About Benny and me."

I creased my brow, not understanding. "Who? Who knows? Someone at Crimson Corp?"

She looked ashamed, and she lowered her eyes. "His wife. His wife knows we were having an affair ... and I think she knows about the Masquerade too."

27

SMALL VICTORIES

ALATHIA

I GOT HOME FEELING SUPREMELY unsettled. I was so on edge that when a car backfired I unholstered my gun and had the safety off before I had even registered what I was doing. I took a breath and slid it back into its black leather brace and pushed through the entrance door. I didn't like the idea of leaving Veronica Jama with her crazy mother; I didn't like it at all. I wasn't afraid of the knife ... I thought that she was physically harmless. But emotionally speaking, untold pain lurked on the family's horizon. I knew firsthand about that kind of turmoil. I pushed the memories down, back into the murk where they belonged. I couldn't think about the ghosts in my past. I couldn't think about my mother. Not then. I needed to focus on finding who killed Benedict.

"Call Samira," I told my phone. It dialed, but there was no answer. My adrenaline spiked. There was something wrong. I knew it, but I didn't know what to do about it. Edgar said Samira hadn't been home when he went to check on her. Hadn't been home since our argument at Crimson Corp. Frustrated, I unlocked my front door with my fingerprint then kicked it open. I liked my silver-toed boots for a lot of reasons, and one of them was that I was able to kick things without hurting my toes. Sometimes it's the small victories.

I didn't have time to act smug, though, because that smell was back. That stranger. The ambitious journalist who was sniffing around the Magnate Club. I froze.

Clearly, he hadn't been content with sliding a note under my door. It wasn't enough of an invasion for him. He had to physically break into my home. Bastard. Men who invade women's spaces in any way really flick my switch, and not in a good way. This time when I pulled my revolver out I did it slowly, silently. I crept in stealth mode, searching the rooms for the intruder, my breath controlled and shallow.

I found him in my personal office, back turned to me, rifling through my drawers. I aimed the revolver at him and cocked it, finger on the trigger. He heard the mechanism and froze.

"Slowly," I said. "Arms up. Turn around. Easy does it."

He did as instructed, and I saw and smell the geysers of sweat underneath his arms. I also noticed the telltale white thumb pad where he was wearing a printed silicone fingerprint. He had gone to a lot of trouble to access my apartment.

"Give me one good reason why I shouldn't shoot you right now."

"I know this must look bad," he said.

"Look bad? You weren't happy with the threatening note you left here last night?"

"It wasn't meant as a threat," he said, but shame darkened his cheeks.

I will report you to the police and blow the Masquerade wide open if you don't meet with me tomorrow.

"Oh," I said. "I must have misunderstood the part about you reporting me to the police."

"I was desperate," he said, his hands still in the air. "I needed to meet you and I knew you wouldn't agree to it."

"So you thought you'd try to blackmail me. Then break into my house," I said.

"Desperate times," he said. "Like you breaking into the Magnate Club."

I pursed my lips. "Now's not the time to be petty."

"I know what you are," he said.

"I'm an accomplished detective with an instinct for blood," I said, finger still on the trigger. "Also, I'm a pretty good shot."

"You're a vampire," he said.

"That's incidental."

"You're an Arcane," he said.

"And you're a muggle who knows too much," I hissed. "Tell me why you're here."

"I know you have the X-Blades."

"Is that what you're looking for? The scissors?"

"The murder weapon." He stared at me as if I was the one who had pinned a grown man to the wall.

"You're crazy," I said, shaking my head.

"You'd be surprised how often I'm called that."

"No," I said. "I wouldn't. You broke into a vampire's house to steal a pair of scissors. Why risk your life for that?"

"I told you in the note. We're on the same side."

"Somehow, I doubt that."

"We have a mutual enemy."

That didn't make him a friend. "Get out," I said.

He cast his eyes up to the ceiling in what I guessed was frustration and defeat, then began to move slowly toward the door.

"I'm going to blow this wide open," he threatened. "People will finally believe me about the Masquerade."

"Suit yourself," I said. "Tell your newspaper all about the mean lady vampire you weren't able to extort. We'll see how that works out for you."

I didn't lower the gun but followed the line of his sagging shoulders till he was out of the front door.

After I slammed it, he shouted through the timber. "You may want to have your security system upgraded," he yelled. "You're not safe here."

28

FULL-BODY CRIMSON

SAMIRA

Neither Alinka nor Lila had to put me out of their safehouse because the moment Lila had dropped *that* intel, I was hauling ass. Crimson Corp hadn't escaped my radar, but the wife had just become my prime murder suspect. As she was still breathing, I needed to get moving and find her.

Before I could leave, though, Lila had given me some baggy old clothes and had urged me to take something. *Two* somethings, actually, that looked like those EpiPen auto-injectors. Said they would help me metabolize the silver faster and ease the pain.

Something she called EverDark.

Even now, as I walked up to the trellis gate of the Jama residence, the capsules bulged in my back pocket. But self-medication was the last thing on my mind.

I stepped closer to the iron trellis, and I knew immediately that Alathia had been here. And not too long ago either. Her scent still lingered in the air.

I did an internal check on the wolf, and a mental whine echoed back to me. She was a little better. Still licking her wounds in her cage, and wouldn't be coming out any time soon, but definitely better. I'd have to rely on my inner human for this round. A better deal, anyway. I had a feeling that Mrs. Jama wouldn't be too fond of werewolves, considering her husband had been cheating with one.

I placed a hand on the gate, figuring out a way in. Would the doorbell be the best choice? A phone call? What *was* the best way to get into someone's house and accuse them of murder?

I smirked at the thought, and as I leaned my weight against the gate, it swung open. Bewildered, I stepped through. The front door of the Jama house was also open. Just enough for a lurking werewolf like me to notice.

Not good. Not good at all.

Gathering my courage, I slipped through the gate and walked up to the residence.

Death was the first thing I smelled. My senses weren't fully restored but even humans were equipped to detect such foul things. The unforgettable scent of freshly butchered meat hung in the air, and I felt only the slightest shame as my mouth watered. I hadn't eaten in over a day ... and, the full moon approached.

Focus, Sami.

The sharp internal reprimand turned my eyes forward and my hearing outward. Too late.

The distant pump of a shotgun resounded through the space, and I leaped, diving behind the nearest couch.

BOOM!

Glass, wood, and fluff exploded into the air. I landed hard, pinpointing the direction the sudden footsteps came from. Whoever it was, was coming for me, but the footsteps were too heavy, too *masculine*—

I rolled into a crouch, picked up the couch that shielded me, and threw it in the direction of the assailant. The second blast ripped through the air. Buckshot tore into the fabric as the couch barreled through the metal wasp cloud—

"ARGH!!"

A satisfying *smack* reverberated as it slammed into the man who'd just stepped into the room. He hit the floor, and his shotgun clattered away from him. Already moving, halving the distance between us, my reflexes were still sluggish.

By the time I reached the kitchen doorway, the man was gone, flying out the back door and through the gardens.

"Yeesh ..." Exhausted, I slumped against the doorway and tried to catch my breath.

A hand protruded from behind the kitchen island. Dark blue tinged its delicately manicured fingers, all of which were frozen in a half-curl.

"Oh no ..."

I re-engaged my nose. The smell of fresh death had been coming from here the entire time.

I swayed to a stand, limped over, and looked.

Wide shining eyes met mine. They screamed for help, or had before the pleas became trapped under the glass of Death. Small cuts, hundreds of them, drew tiger stripes across her skin; the blood seeped from the wounds to create a full-body crimson gel, as though someone had dipped her in dark paint and left her on the floor to dry.

But the cuts were child's play compared to the multiple stab wounds in her chest, crowned by the large butcher knife lodged in her heart.

Mrs. Jama.

Some sick piece of shit, likely the man I'd just let escape, had tortured the poor woman before he'd killed her. And from the way her husband had been handled, I knew in my gut that their murderer had been one and the same.

29

A LIFE SENTENCE IS A LONG TIME WHEN
YOU'RE A VAMPIRE

ALATHIA

THANKS FOR THAT. Telling me I wasn't safe in my own home and then buggering off. Not that I wanted the journalist to stay—he gave me the creeps—but I couldn't shake the feeling that he was right. As much as I didn't want to form an alliance with him, I agreed that he knew more than was good for him. Whether I liked it or not, we would have to work together to get to the bottom of whatever was going on.

I needed to find Samira, but I didn't know where to start. Where did she go after our disagreement at Crimson Corp? Red Kite? The primordial Vampire Kinship? I doubted it. Knowing Sami, she'd start with the most interesting lead she had, which was the scent of wolf on Benedict Jama's body. But I didn't know the particulars of the Lycana hangouts in Jozi, so that didn't help me much.

I pulled off my boots, poured myself a vodka on the rocks, and padded through to my ransacked office. I didn't bother tidying it. My laptop was open, but I saw with some satisfaction that the journo hadn't managed to crack the code.

Otac, I typed. It meant "dad" in Croatian. A reminder popped up that I had a new phone contact. Would I like to add it to my other lists?

Damn right I would. I inspected the photos of the X-Blades that Vale had sent me. Without even thinking about it, I typed a text to him. It wasn't a phrase I was given to using, but as the journalist creep had said, desperate times. I took a large sip of vodka and tapped "send."

I need help.

It took five sips before the wizard saw my message and replied. *You in trouble? Tell me where.*

I pulled off my boots and pulled my knees up to my chest.

Not in trouble, I typed. *Not yet, anyway.*

Not true, he replied. *I know trouble when I see it.*

I laughed. He was right.

Do you still have your job? I typed.

I returned the X-Blades, he said. *The Museum was very grateful.*

Good, I replied, and chose the relieved emoji.

He typed while I waited, a fluttering in my stomach. Geeky wizards weren't usually my type, but I'd had an instant physical connection with Vale. Finally, his message came through. *What do you need help with?*

I took a breath. *You have access to the Arcane Dark Web, right?*

You're not supposed to know about that.

I know, I replied. *I've been trying to hack it for years.*

You'll be prosecuted if they catch you.

They won't catch me.

A prison life sentence is a long time when you're a vampire.

LOL, I typed, adding a laughing emoji.

He sent me the handcuffs emoji and I felt a thrill zipping up my spine. I didn't think he was being kinky, but I couldn't help picturing us playing with the cuffs.

Don't tempt me, I typed.

My phone rang, startling me. I almost dropped it.

"Holy hex," I said, picking up. "You gave me a fright."

"By phoning?" Vale said. "You're full of surprises."

"I wasn't expecting it to ring, that's all. I'm on edge. It's been an ... interesting day."

"You're telling me," he said.

My body relaxed into the chair as I held the phone close to my ear.

"I called because we shouldn't risk exchanging dark web stuff over text. It's not safe."

"Of course," I said. "I was expecting you to just say no and then ghost me."

"No, you weren't," he said.

"No, I wasn't," I said, smiling into the receiver.

"What do you need to know?"

"There's a human I need to track down. A man. A doomsday prepper. I'm assuming he has an Arcane profile because he's a danger to the Masquerade. He hangs around Crimson Corp and threatens to bomb the place. Says he knows about the Arcanes. The other humans think his conspiracies are crazy, but one day someone will believe him—"

If the prepper ever crossed paths with the journalist, we'd have a problem on our hands.

"You have a name?" Vale asked.

"Malcolm Beukes. Obviously not his real name."

"That's not helpful."

"I have a photo." I sent the photo of the prepper to Vale's phone so that he could run it through the database. "This is what the CEO of Crimson Corp gave me. It looks like he's climbing into a taxi at the Sandton depot. It's dated two weeks ago."

"Hmm," he said. "That's interesting."

"What now?"

"No match."

"Why is that interesting?"

"Because it's impossible. The ADWD has every single person's profile on it, including facial features, fingerprints, blood type, Arcane species—"

"It's a mask," I said.

"Yes."

"One of those high-tech ones with animated pixels."

"Looks like it."

"I'll put my money on the fact that this isn't the only trouble this guy is causing. Can you run that particular mask for other complaints?"

"Hang on," he said, and I heard him hammering on his keyboard. "Bingo."

"I'm listening."

"Eighty-four hits from all over the city. And that's just in the last few months. Making threats. Waving weapons. Vandalizing walls and bill-boards. Setting fire to monuments."

"Busy guy," I said.

"That's assuming, of course, that he's the only one going around in this kind of mask. There may be more of them. It might be an organized movement."

"What can you tell me about the mask?"

"It's smart, but not smart enough to fool the AI profiler."

"Would you run a search for the mask without narrowing the results to criminal activity?"

"You're saying he'd wear his mask to walk down to the local shops to buy a pack of smokes?"

"Just run it," I said.

If he was as paranoid as I thought he was, he'd always wear his mask. And every time he went to lift weights at the gym, went shopping, visited the cinema, the security cameras would have tracked him.

My phone beeped with a notification. It was the map of the prepper's movements, and it looked like a beautiful spirograph. Existing theory suggested he would live in the middle of the pattern. I zoomed in. Emmarentia. Helpful, but how would I narrow it down?

"Any chance of a credit card purchase?" I asked.

"Nope."

Of course, the guy was too loco to trust banks.

"Uber?"

"We can hack that," he said. There was more crunching of keys. "I'll triangulate the footage of him climbing into the taxi in Sandton two weeks ago with Uber's records."

I waited, tapping my bare foot on the polished timber floor.

"Yes," he said. "Got the street address."

"Yes!" I said.

"Hang on," he said. "Now that we have his address, we can backtrack for his real identity."

Jaysus, you're sexy, I wanted to say. But I held back. We had a rogue prepper to track down.

"Got it," he said, then stopped. "Wait, what?"

"What?" I asked.

"He's a ... professor?"

"You sure you have the right guy?"

"Listen to this. Expert in chemical engineering—"

"Is that code for bomb-making?"

"Yes."

"Also, he has *cum laude* degrees in supernatural sciences and a background in collecting magical artifacts."

What I didn't say aloud: Every time I see the phrase *cum laude* I think it sounds like a sex instruction. I smiled and cleared my throat.

"Those degrees are not offered at a regular university."

"Exactly. It's as though he lives just under the surface of the Masquerade."

I pictured the prepper behind a thin curtain that billowed in a breeze. Now you see him, now you don't.

"Looks like we have our guy," I said.

Violent? Check. Paranoid? Check. Crazy enough to steal a pair of magical scissors and stab a capitalist with them? Check.

A little flame of excitement sparked in my stomach. We had him.

"You can't go after him on your own," he said.

"Oh yes, I can."

I heard a noise at the door. I was about to say something to Vane, but the call had been disconnected.

30

DEAD ENDS, PEEPING TOMS, AND BROKEN PROMISES

SAMIRA

I'D GATHERED everything I needed before I called the police. It hadn't been easy collecting evidence from a crime scene without actually taking it, but such was the life of a paranormal P.I. You had to take what you could get and fill in the blanks while stupid humans could take *all* they wanted and still not solve the case.

But I'd managed.

I'd done an entire sniff-down of the scene and had taken notes. Had found a camera in the little girl's room and had taken pictures. Had thanked the gods she was still at school ... for obvious reasons. Had used a crapload of Scotch tape and baby powder to take some crude prints. Wouldn't work for human eyes, but they'd work just fine for mine. Once I was back at 100% that was. I'd taken prints off the man's shotgun and the butcher knife. Had taken samples from Mrs. Jama's fingernails. She'd fought for her life, sadly, and though she'd lost the fight, thanks to her I wouldn't lose the trail.

Such were the downsides of murdering psychopaths ... They *loved* to fap off to the bloodshed, but they were often sloppy and left a mess of traceables.

I was determined to catch the psychotic bastard who'd done this.

The house phone was now off the hook. And the police were on their way. Time to go. I took one last look at Mrs. Jama. My heart twisted.

"Your life sucked. And I don't know why. But I'll find out, I promise."

Leaving the same way my murder suspect had, I stepped out of the back of the house. And as I stepped down into the garden, I noticed it: the flash of light in the distance, and the drawing of curtains.

Someone was watching the house. And they'd just gotten a picture of me leaving a murder scene.

Faster than you could say "Peeping Tom," I was at the offender's house, because despite my fatigue, I was ready to rip the camera from his grip and take his hands too. I knocked, loudly. No answer.

I didn't wait for an invitation.

Breaking the door off its hinges, I barged in,—holy hell, I must be healing faster than I thought—and I stalked into the house. In the distance I heard a shriek, punctuated by the wooden scrape of a window opening, and I swept through the house, homing in on my prey—er, *target*—like a bee to honey. As he dove out the window, I grabbed his leg and dragged him back in.

The poor kid, he couldn't have been any older than nineteen, screamed and shrieked. Like a little girl. It was actually kind of funny. "OH CHRIST, PLEASE DON'T KILL ME!"

I raised a brow. "I'm a detective. I don't kill people. But if you thought I was capable of that, then you're an idiot for snapping photos of me. And you were dumb enough to use a flash, in broad daylight? Do you even *deserve* to live?"

"I wasn't trying to snap you, I was trying to—well—" And suddenly he got sheepish. His eyes tried desperately *not* to look at the walls around him, so I took a look for him.

Oh, GROSS.

The walls, and the floors for that matter, were messy, filled with pin-ups from unsavory publications like *Hustler* and *Maxim*. But interspersed with the mags were pictures. Endless pictures of Mrs. Jama. Of her coming out of her house, of her bending over to water her begonias, of her sunbathing in her backyard.

While this kid clearly wasn't the leader of the neighborhood crime watch, he *was* a total pervert. The peeping Tom even kept plenty of tissue and lotion stashed. Rows and rows of it. Boy could have opened his own bodega. He deserved a good ass whipping, and my eyes said as much because when I turned back to him, he cowered on the floor.

"Please, please don't tell my folks!"

"That you're a peeping Tom who jacks off to rich cougar neighbor ladies? Not interested, kid." I looked away, more relieved than I want to reveal. If this kid had been someone trying to frame me, I would have been screwed ...

My eyes widened as an opportunity dawned on me.

"Hey, kid. How long have you been taking pictures of Mrs. Jama?"

"I... I dunno. Maybe for about ..." He cringed, embarrassed. "Three months?"

This kid may have just saved the day after all.

"How about we make a deal? You give me all your pictures. Your camera, your thumb drive ... *everything* with Mrs. Jama on it, and I won't tell the cops you've been, oh how do we say this in law enforcement? *Criminally stalking* her."

His face deflated in terror. Jackpot.

"Oh my God, I don't wanna go to jail. PLEASE don't send me to jail!"

"Then hand over your data. Hand over *everything*."

The boy scrambled, whisking pictures off his walls like a whirlwind. He shook them out of his bedsheets, mined them from his desk drawers, and even snatched them from his backpack.

Yeesh. This kid was going to have a weirdo adult life. He probably *should* go see someone, so that he didn't turn into a 50-year-old pervert, but hey. I could only save the world one crazy at a time. So I decided to let it go.

In the next few minutes, everything he'd ever gathered on Mrs. Jama and her house was stuffed inside a shoebox in my arms. Including his three cameras, thumb drives, and backups. Then on my command, he completely cleaned out his computer. When he was done, his face was beaded with sweat. There were some tears mixed in too, but I pretended not to notice. He'd already embarrassed himself enough.

"I won't turn you in, and I won't tell your folks. Not unless I come back here and find more pics, that is."

"Oh thank you, THANK YOU!"

I nodded and turned to leave. Then I stopped, wondering if I should. I turned back to him, my face soft. "Kid ... do you remember seeing anyone around the Jamas's house other than her husband, her, and her kid?"

He thought for a minute, hard. Then he brightened. "Actually, yeah! There was this guy, tall, kinda mysterious. Never saw him until a couple of weeks ago. Thought for a while that he and Mrs. Jama were ... you know ..." He made a hole with his thumb and forefinger and stuck his other finger through it. Several times.

I made a face. "Yeah, I get your point, kid."

"But if they were, he must have been some hired gigolo or something, because he never hugged her or kissed her or anything. Not like a side lover might, you know? I thought maybe she just paid him for a sausage poke now and again."

"Did you get any pictures of him?" I put my hand on the shoebox lid, indicating the data inside.

He shook his head. "Nah. I wasn't interested in who or what the Mrs. was doing. I was just ... into *her*."

Clearly.

"And did you get to see the face of this man?"

"No, that was always the weird thing. Whenever I'd look at him through my camera's viewfinder, I'd only see a weird shimmer on his face."

"A shimmer?"

"Yeah! Like a layer of light, or ... something. Have no clue what it was, but there was no way my camera was going to pick up on anything but, like, a sheet of sparkles, or whatever." He thought for a moment. "You know, kind of like those sparkly vampires in that book—"

"Yeah, I get it, kid." I shifted. Even the mere mention of fictional depictions of the Masquerade made me uncomfortable. Humans getting too close and all.

"Except shinier. Like it was designed to throw off detection."

This was a gold mine of information. If this kid wasn't such a pervert and I didn't have to avoid him on full moons, I'd even consider hiring him. He'd make one hell of an investigator.

"Thanks, kid. You've been a major help. I'll keep up my end of our deal."

His mousy voice stopped me as I turned to leave. "Oh, um. And Mrs. Jama? She's ... she's a really nice lady. Lonely. But really nice. I don't want her to, you know, think anything bad about me. She's the only person in the neighborhood who really looks out for me, you know? So, you won't tell Mrs. Jama either, right?"

My back was to him, and thank God it was, because I cringed, feeling sadness twist my guts into knots. Between the dead ends, peeping Toms, and empty promises? This day had been trash.

Holding back the tears, I took a breath. "Don't worry, kid," I said shakily. "Trust me. I won't tell her a thing."

31

DADDY DOOMSDAY

ALATHIA

"Samira!" I shouted as she fell through the doorway.

Where the hell have you been? I wanted to yell, but she wasn't in good shape.

"What happened to you?"

Sami looked at me with those feral eyes of hers and all the pain in them. She held up a hand. I noticed a shoebox balanced in the other. "I'm fine."

"You don't look fine! What the hell?"

I wanted to scold her for not answering her phone, but then I saw the ligature marks on her wrists. If she'd been tied up, she wouldn't have been able to answer her phone, even if she had wanted to. I tried to help her over to the sofa, but she swatted me away.

"You're injured," I said. "Or ... sick?"

"Not for long," she replied and lowered herself onto the chaise longue. Her rapid healing would kick in—if it hadn't already—and she'd be back to normal. I hoped. I fetched water and set the glass down on the table beside her.

"God," she said, covering her face with her hands and shaking her head. "I've got so much to tell you."

"I've also got something," I said. "You go first."

She took a deep breath, as though preparing for the plunge into Hell. Still, she forced a smile. "Okay! So. I went wolf."

"Okay."

"And I ... buried my phone."

"You *what*?" Immediately, my understanding fizzled into anger. The idiot hadn't been too tied up to answer my calls after all. She'd just stupidly abandoned her cell altogether. Had she lost her mind?

She saw my simmering rage and pushed on nervously. "Aaaannnd I infiltrated a club while naked, saw that prepper guy, destroyed an illegal Lycana sex ring, freed a few wolves into the wild, roughed up a few vampires, got shot with silver, met Jama's baby mama, thought the wife was his killer—and she still might *be* his killer—*Matrix*-dodged an assassin with a shotgun, found Mrs. Jama murdered with a butcher knife, and then shook one of her nosy, perverted neighbors down for info!"

What? There was way too much information swirling around the room, but I couldn't think about it. All I could picture was poor Veronica Jama, who had now had both her parents taken from her. Violently, in cold blood. I just stared at Samira while my brain whirred.

She took a deep breath and smiled at me widely. "And I stopped for some calming chai on the way back. So! How was *your* evening?" And the fool batted her eyelashes at me, as though we were at a ladies' luncheon at the Jo'burg Country Club.

. . .

Still traumatized by the news of Mrs. Jama, I spoke slowly. As I got into it, I picked up the pace and told her everything as quickly as I could. About the prepper's mask, his criminal charges, the chemical engineering degree, the obsession with Arcanes and magical artifacts. Despite separate investigations, our findings pointed in the same direction.

"Yeah. The kid told me a guy hanging around Mrs. Jama's place wore a uniform. I dunno, maybe military fatigues? So it could be him," she said. "Daddy Doomsday."

"Okay. But I think you should rest now. We'll go in the morning."

Her eyes flared and glittered. "I don't want him hurting anyone else. That psycho bastard not only killed Mrs. Jama, but he tortured her beforehand. This woman died screaming." Then she paused, sudden pain in her face. "He ran right by me, Alla." She squeezed her eyes shut. "I could have stopped him on my way into the club, but I let him go. Can't you see? If I had stopped him, Mrs. Jama would still be alive."

"You ..." I said. "You're not well enough. You need to regain your strength."

"Plenty of time for that," she replied. Her resolve made her look stronger, and she wiped her mouth and stood up, limber and proud. "I want this lunatic off the streets before he hurts anyone else."

"We do have his home address," I mused. "It would be a shame not to use it."

Samira smiled. That crazy wolf smile she reserved for special occasions. I pulled my boots back on and my jacket. Grabbed my keys.

I pictured Veronica again, pale-skinned, wide-eyed, saying that she didn't believe in magic.

"Let's go."

32

KITTENS AND KAPOODLES

SAMIRA

"Yeesh, this place is a sty," I muttered.

Alla elbowed me into silence as we stepped into the prepper's apartment. I use the word "apartment" loosely because it looked more like a landfill from where I stood. Even in the dark, I could see crazy plastered all over the walls and floor. Photos, dossiers, maps, those string connector things à la *A Beautiful Mind* ... I mean ... WOW.

My nose took in the evaporated swill of a hot mess life: aging Chinese food in the garbage, old moldy socks, underwear smelling of male butt crack, and ... dog food?

"Think he made a break for it," I whispered. "Can't hear or smell him *anywhere.*"

Alla nodded, but she pulled her revolver anyway. She trusted my senses, but she also trusted her gat. It would tie up any loose ends that might come careening around a corner at any second.

I walked further into the room, and as I did, my foot grazed a plastic bottle. It crackled emptily as it rolled away from me. My eyes saw what Alla's couldn't: it was an empty King Malta. A South African malt drink. And by the light smell of mint gum emanating from it, the prepper had consumed it only 30 minutes ago.

A blink of light inside the bottle, a high whine, and then—

"ALLA, GET DOWN!" I threw my bomber jacket over her face as I tackled her, twisting so that her body faced away from the bottle.

A pale shock of light cracked through the room. UV light.

We hit the floor, and just as I was getting up, I heard the metallic *clack* of a shotgun being racked. I threw Alla to the left and dashed to the right as the shotgun blast tore into the air between us and clipped the front door, blowing part of it into splinters.

My skin sizzled as a familiar dust sprinkled into the air. Silver. The gunpowder was laced with silver. I rolled out of range and kipped up to my feet just in time to see a shadowy figure disappear behind the kitchen wall.

"WHO THE HELL ARE YOU?!" he shrieked. "GET OUT OF MY HOUSE!"

I tensed, ready to spring. On the other side of me, Alla was getting to her feet. She ripped the jacket off her head, lifted her gun, and aimed forward into the darkness, her fangs bared. She was pissed.

"You're under arrest for the murder of Benjamin Jama!" I snapped. "Drop the gun and come out with your hands up!"

"Murder?! You think it was *me* who killed that guy?! You're crazy!"

"Well, show us we're wrong, sir, and drop the gun."

"You're in *my* house, and I don't have to drop *shit*! Show me your warrant first!"

I winced. Oops. Yeeeah, sort of forgot about that part.

As though he could read my mind, Daddy Doomsday sneered. "I

knew it. You liars, you're not cops. You're the Arcane Gestapo trying to shut me up! I *knew* you'd be here one day, *all* of you, trying to frame me! Trying to take me down because I know the truth!"

I raised an eyebrow, and Alla and I exchanged glances. But while I was downright perplexed, the look on her face was one of recognition. She signaled for me to keep talking, and she furrowed her brow, straining to listen.

"The truth?" I asked. "The truth about what?"

"I saw you at Wolfsbane. I know you. I know what you are! All of you!"

Alla cocked her head, still listening hard.

"Yeah. We're a couple of PIs who are about to stomp your ass and haul you off to prison," I growled. "Put the gun down. NOW. You have three seconds. One!"

"Like hell I will! I'm going to blow your little Masquerade wide open or die trying!"

"Two!" I was already halfway across the room, and even through the wall between us, I heard his sweat-slimed fingers tighten around the shottie. I had to take this guy out, no question.

"STAY AWAY FROM ME!" he screamed, frantic. "I'M WARNING YOU!"

"Thr—"

"Hey," Alla said finally. "You. Muggle who knows too much."

The rapid breathing behind the wall suddenly slowed down, and I heard his clothes rubbing against the paint as he relaxed. "Alathia?"

I also saw her relax a bit, but she never eased her stance. She kept the gun aimed. "Yeah, it's me. Will you come out?"

My eyes widened. Alathia knew the killer? I looked at her and frowned. "This isn't an ex-boyfriend, is it?"

She scowled at me and turned her attention back to Daddy Doomsday. "Come out. We won't hurt you. We just want to talk."

"Are you going to put your gun down?" His voice quivered. "Are you going to tell the wolf to back off?"

"No. I'm not. But if you don't try anything crazy, I promise we won't kill you."

Silence.

I was shocked when he did it, but he finally peeked his head around the corner. His hair was frazzled, his eyes were bloodshot, and his chin was grizzled and unshaven. Clearly, this guy wasn't military because he'd just given Alla an A1 shot at his dome. Upon seeing her, though, the rest of his body slunk around the wall. His shotgun rested in his hands, his finger off the trigger.

"Thank you," Alathia said gently. "Mister ...?"

"Malcolm. Malcolm Beukes. And I don't care *what* you heard—" He glared at me, eyes hard. "I did *not* kill Benjamin Jama. He was my only source on the conspiracy."

I frowned, and as I listened to Beukes' words, an omen settled in my belly. Almost in tandem, Aikan's words rose up from the graveyard of my mind and joined Beukes's haunting liturgy.

"What conspiracy?" I asked.

Malcolm set his gaze with mine, dead serious. "The Crimson Corp conspiracy to take over the world."

I sniffed Malcolm over once. Then twice. He didn't like it much, but it was the only way either of us would hear him and his story out. And my nose gave the verdict: Malcolm "Daddy Doomsday" Beukes was *not* the murderer of the Jamas. Whoever this guy was, he didn't smell a bit like the crime scene that'd been left in our office just 40 hours before. Nor did he smell anything like the man who'd killed Mrs. Jama in her kitchen. He was clean, and apparently—

"He's a journalist," Alathia informed me. She cut him with her eyes. "A very *persistent* one at that. He broke into my apartment a little while ago, and was snooping around for leads."

"*WHAT?*" I was already up, ready to throttle him. Alla grabbed my arm.

"I'm sure Malcolm has an explanation. *Many* explanations." She turned to him, her eyes glinting in the dark. "About why he's creeping around Crimson Corp and their properties, his obsession with Arcanes, his penchant for breaking and entering, this 'conspiracy' he and Jama were trying to expose ... *yes?*"

Malcolm looked away, rubbing his arm bashfully. But he nodded. And explain everything, he did. Yes, he *was* a prepper, and he was also the ex-professor journalist who broke into Alathia's place. He believed in the existence of the Arcanes, and he'd been tracking us for years. He knew we were hiding out amongst the humans, and that we were up to no good.

"*Some* of us," I hissed, correcting him. "*Some* of us are up to no good. Just like humans. We might not be like you, but we're not all the same either, Pukes."

"It's *Beukes*," he said, frowning.

"Whatever."

"Where does Benny Jama come into this, Malcolm?" Alathia interrupted calmly.

Malcolm sighed. "Jama and I had gotten into quite a few tussles in the past. He worked the late shifts, and sometimes he'd come out for a smoke or a walk around the Crimson Corp trails and spot me. You know, snooping." He shrugged, bashful. "He'd always call security, always chase me off. But then, one night, he suddenly became less ... uptight. He seemed upset. Haunted. Saw me and didn't say a thing. Just turned the other way and let me look around. Then one day, he came *here*. To my place."

Alathia and I exchanged glances as the new information poured in. We both leaned forward, anxious.

"How did he find you?" Alathia urged.

"I have NO idea!" Malcolm's knuckles went white as he gripped his khaki shorts. "Which freaked me out because if he knew where I lived, that meant Crimson Corp did too, you know? So obviously, I stick the gun in his face to try to make him leave. But he won't. The man is terrified. He says he has a story for me. The story of a lifetime about Crimson Corp, about the Masquerade, about a dark conspiracy going on, about *everything*. Murders, disappearances, experiments. And that he wants *me* to break it. He said he needed to get some things done first, but to meet him at the Origins Museum the next day, 8 p.m. *sharp*. And he'd tell me everything."

"And? What happened after that?" I was practically jumping out of my seat.

"He never showed up." Then he lifted his eyes to us. They were wide and haunted. "Well, he *did* show up, I suppose. But he showed up in your office. Dead."

I sat back and breathed out long and loud. "Wow. That's heavy. So there it is. The whole sack of kittens and kapoodles."

Alla and Malcolm looked at me as though I was insane.

"You mean the whole kit and caboodle," Malcolm corrected me, a sudden smirk on his face. "Right?"

I smiled bashfully and scratched my head. "Oh yeah! Oops! Guess I'm a little hungry."

The growing warmth on his face turned cold, and he looked at me with horror. Guess it was easy for humans to forget what I was when I wasn't furry and tearing people's limbs off. Now freshly reminded, he scooted away.

"So ... that means ... you two *didn't* kill him?" He eyed me, still wary.

"Of course not!" Alla and I snapped together, and as I smugly folded my arms, she took the lead.

"Someone put Jama's body in our office," she explained. "To get our attention and to drag us into this mess. And since you've been making yourself extremely visible during this investigation, Crimson Corp put you at the top of their suspect list."

"Which would make sense if they wanted to throw us a red herring and cover their asses while they keep, what did Jama say?" I grumbled. "Killing people? Disappearing people? Experimenting on people? And then getting *away* with it?"

The very thought pissed me off. The fact that Sullivan had used us and sent us on a wild goose chase while he skipped off scot-free into the sunset? Oh yeah, that pissed me off even more. I got to my feet and clenched my fists.

Inside my waves of anger, though, crosscurrents of nausea *also* hit me. I blinked and shook my head, trying to knock out the sudden blur muddling my vision. Somehow, suddenly, it took everything in me to not keel over. Ugh. I hadn't fully recovered from the silver, I guess, and my body was suffering from its lack of opportunity to heal.

Still? I was ready to kick some Crimson ass.

33

SERVES ME RIGHT FOR BEING BEST FRIENDS WITH A WEREWOLF

ALATHIA

"No, Sami. No. You can't. It's too dangerous."

She flashed her lupine eyes at me. The prepper stood by, silent, bouncing on his toes as if he were anxiously awaiting the beginning of a race.

"It's the only way," said Samira. "Don't you see? Sullivan pointed us in the direction of this loon—no offense—"

Malcolm nodded.

"—pointed us in the direction of Daddy Doomsday here to throw us off the scent. He didn't want us sniffing around Crimson Corp because he's hiding something. Something big."

"That may be so—" I granted.

"So we have no alternative but to find out what it is."

"That's not true," I said. "We can go to the Conclave with this."

Sami looked like I had just told her a joke in Croatian. "Really? The Conclave? Sirela? The same chick who went cray-cray on payday?"

I understood her reluctance. The head of the Arcane governing council, also known as the Nine Cloud Conclave, was a nasty piece of work. According to local lore, the power of being appointed the top wizard in the country had gone to her head, and there were stories of her painting the interior of the Dragon Tower in real gold, and getting her staff encrusted with diamonds. She kicked out all the respected wizards and replaced them with yea-saying lackeys. And that was only the beginning. The other rumors were a lot worse. Of course, plebeians like Samira and I wouldn't know if the stories were true. No one ever got an invitation to the Dragon Tower. Not unless they were forcibly there to receive a death sentence.

"First of all, she's a madwoman," said Samira.

"So we've heard," I said.

"Secondly, she's impossible to contact."

"There will be a way," I said. "There always is."

Vane might know something about gaining access to the tower. He may know one of the wizard interns they have studying under the gray beards.

"And thirdly," Sami huffed, "she'd have us executed just for looking in her direction."

"Really?" said Malcolm, eyebrows lifting. "I've heard whispers about this Sirela lady before, but—"

I cut him off. "Those are all just rumors," I said. "Anyway, we *have* to tell the Conclave. This is bigger than Benedict Jama, and it's bigger than us."

"If we tell the council," said Samira. "You know what will happen. Damon Sullivan will get wind of it before they even start the investigation, and he'll be out of here and setting up shop somewhere else with a new name and a new face and more innocent victims to kill."

"That's not ideal—"

Samira scoffed.

"That's not ideal," I said again, "but it's better than you going in there and getting yourself killed."

"Damn it, Alla!" yelled Samira. "Don't you want to know what's going on in there?"

"Of course I do!"

"So. Damn. Stubborn!"

"I'm stubborn?"

We stood in tense silence for a moment, and then Samira shook her head. "You're cold, you know that?"

Malcolm blinked his beady eyes, looked worried. Was he going to witness a vamp-wolf deathmatch?

My jaw clenched. "What? Where did that come from? What does that even mean?"

She shook her head again. "You're willing to just let this whole thing go because it's become inconvenient to you."

I gasped. "I'm not!"

"And you can go back to your safe million-dollar apartment and pay no attention to the wretched people on the ground who are being targeted by the unethical pathological capitalist assholes like Sullivan."

"Listen, Sami—"

"No!" she growled. "No. I'm tired of listening. I'm going to take action. I'm going to bring Crimson Corp down, or I'm gonna die trying."

"Please," I begged. I couldn't stand the idea of her going in there alone, but I wouldn't go with her. I knew it was a suicide mission. I loved Samira deeply, but I would not sacrifice my life because she'd all of a sudden decided to be a kamikaze. You don't get to live to be three hundred by making rash decisions like that. Besides, what was the point in finding out what was under Crimson Corp's bonnet if we weren't going to live to tell the tale?

I'd ask her one more time to reconsider. My plan was to ply her with some delicious food and a good rest before taking on any evil villains, then slowly work on changing her mind, but before I opened my mouth, she had hightailed it out of the door. Malcolm just blinked at me. I sighed and sagged down onto his disgusting sofa, hands covering my face. My head pounded in my palms. I knew that if I didn't follow her, it would be the last time I saw her alive.

I couldn't let that happen. I couldn't let her go in there alone. Her first memory was being abandoned as a pup. I couldn't let that be her last moment, too.

Anger bubbled inside me, but also a sense of purpose. Would I have to die because of her hot-headedness? Probably. Ah, well. I guess three centuries is a good inning. I hauled a deep breath into my lungs and stood up. So much for self-preservation. Served me right for being best friends with a werewolf.

"Well," I said to Malcolm. "Are you coming?"

"It's a suicide mission," he said. "Those guards shoot first and ask questions later."

"Is that a yes?"

Malcolm rubbed the stubble on his chin. "I guess so."

I walked out of his bunker and he followed me. I moved quickly over his messy garden, tripping over carrot tops and sweet potato vines.

Can't trust the grocers nowadays, I imagined him saying. *Chem trails. Hidden toxins. GMOs.*

I didn't want to spend too much time with the guy—didn't want his brand of crazy to rub off on me—but at the same time, it was nice to have a sidekick, even if said sidekick happened to be one crayon short of a box. I almost stumbled over a cabbage and swore under my breath about his paranoia almost breaking my ankle. I was happy to escape the organic pesticide-free jungle and get my boots onto the hard concrete slab of the sidewalk outside his property. As uneven as it was, it was better than being tripped by organic garden produce.

My Jaguar looked especially good parked on the other side of the street, just shy of the lone, flickering street lamp, gleaming and purring. Edgar would take us to Crimson Corp, we'd get Samira and whatever intel we could gather from Benedict Jama's office, and the case would be wrapped.

"I'm not getting in that car," said Doomsday.

I stopped in the middle of the road and turned to look at him. The darkness of night seemed to swirl around us. "What? Why?"

"I don't get into cars with strangers," he said, his arms by his sides.

My exasperation made me hiss at him. "What are you? Five?"

He shrugged and looked at me as if I had the answers to the great questions of the universe. Like a baby duck looks at his momma duck. I sighed. "Just get in the car."

"No," he said, shaking his head. The light flickered, threatening to go off altogether.

"He's not a stranger," I said. "He's my chauffeur. His name is Edgar. He's eighty in the shade. What exactly do you think he's going to do to you? Crack you on the skull with his walker?"

Malcolm peered at me, not convinced.

"You've taken taxis before," I said. "I've seen you!"

"That's a driver I know. Not a stranger."

"Well, Edgar is my driver. Are you coming?"

He shook his head. I felt like kicking him. Literally.

"I'm getting in the car now. Are you coming or staying?"

"I'm coming," he said.

Relief.

"But I'm not getting in that car."

I ground my teeth, my jaw muscles aching from the tension of the day.

"Fine," I said, spinning to face the growling car. "I'll see you there. When it's all over."

Asshole.

Irritation with Samira and Malcolm like stones in my shoes, I marched toward the Jag. Why did I always get saddled with the stupid ones? My nails bit into my palms and forced me to relax. Arriving at Crimson feeling like I was about to explode would not help anyone. I had to chill. I had to breathe. The car door popped open, and I climbed in gratefully.

As the car pulled off, I leaned heavily against the backrest and closed my eyes. "To Crimson Corp, please, Edgar," I said, massaging the knots in my shoulders. "And will you play some of that classical music?"

When he didn't respond, my eyes clicked open. I looked at the driver. It wasn't Edgar.

34

MURDER MYSTERY THEATER

SAMIRA

THE TREK to the Crimson Corp grounds took a heavier toll on my body than usual. I'd turned wolf for the ease and speed of travel, and I'd gotten neither. I didn't even make it there before I had to stop and rest by the road.

My usually powerful limbs felt like jelly, and shocks of sleek black hair fell from my coat in clumps. My jaws, which carried the clothes I'd just been wearing ten minutes before, slackened. Worse, it was getting harder to force them closed: they felt out of my control.

Man ... and just when I thought I was getting better.

My body was still fighting the silver poisoning, but not quickly enough. Alla was right; I needed rest, and I hadn't listened, and now the silver was going to take me out.

My body forced me back into human form, and I slumped against a nearby tree, breathing hard. It was a struggle to get my clothes back on, but I did. Thankfully, the road nearby was both privately owned by Crimson Corp *and* was relatively low-traffic. Most of Crimson's employees had already arrived at work, and I couldn't be happier about it. The only thing worse than dying here would have been to die here naked, with my bare ass in the air.

I jammed my hand into my back pocket, remembering the EverDark pen. I took it out and slammed it into my thigh.

Then I crumpled to the ground.

My eyes fluttered, and fatigue swept over me, taking my consciousness with it. But before I went out completely, I heard the whisper of bending grass. Footsteps. Then the voice.

"Hello, Samira."

The smooth, husky voice that stroked the air was almost a little more than I could handle right now, but I kept cool. I had no choice but to keep cool, really, but that was beside the point.

"I was wondering if I should worry," the voice continued. "And by the sight of you, it's clear I should've started worrying hours ago."

I fell to the side, but two hands caught me, hoisted me up over a strong, broad shoulder. I was fading, but I smelled him, the scent of soap on his skin, the familiar tinge of cinnamon. I smelled Aikan ... and it was a scent that lulled me to sleep as he carried me away.

"ALLA!"

Aikan had to shove an arm in front of me to keep me from leaping out of bed when I woke up screaming and reaching. I breathed heavily, and my body dripped with sweat.

"Hey," Aikan's low and soft voice grabbed my attention. I looked at him, the fiery gold of his gaze reflected at me, even in the dark. "It's okay. Just relax, all right? You were dreaming."

I blinked, the demons of my sleep dissipating before my eyes. "Jesus

..." I put my face in my hands. "Feels like I've been hit by a Mack truck."

"A truck would have been kinder to you. You've got the silver fevre, a far more dangerous adversary. You need to rest."

I shook my head and tried to get up. "But I have to—"

"It's not a request!" he snapped suddenly, and the snarl inside his voice sealed my lips. "You almost killed yourself out there!"

My eyes widened, and I looked at him, shocked. It's true, for werewolves the "silver fevre" was just as dangerous as silver poisoning. It was a sort of sepsis only we could get, an immunological overreaction our bodies experienced when trying to rid themselves of poison. For many of us, it was the fevre, or "fever," that killed us. Sometimes even faster than the poisoning itself. The key to beating it was more fluids, dialysis, and rest. None of which I could afford right now.

But Aikan seemed insistent. He looked downright violent, as though he was prepared to make me stay here by force. I cocked my head, curious. We barely knew each other. Why did he seem so ... invested?

He saw me looking at him, saw the question on my face, and he tore his eyes away. "What do you have to report?" He muttered.

I scoffed. "Report? To *you*, you mean? Nothing. Especially because I don't work for you."

Aikan rubbed the bridge of his nose. He was already tired of me, but I didn't care.

"We're barely even partners," I continued. "So no, you don't need to bother your pretty little head with my whereabouts."

He chuckled. "Barely even partners, but we *are* in bed together, Samira."

"Then your foreplay is trash," I snapped evenly. "I've been through literal hell to find Jama's killer. Where the hell have *you* been? What do I get from you in return?"

"Me saving your life for one. And for two, these." He reached under the bed and pulled something out. It was my cell phone. And my clothes from hours before. I'd buried them, and he'd somehow been able to retrieve them. He turned the phone on, and immediately I heard the dinging of messages. Countless messages.

"I've been trying to reach you." He frowned at me and tossed the phone into my lap.

"Oh yeah?" I tossed the phone to the side. "Well, I'm here now. What do you want?"

"An update, obviously."

"And why would I give information to a Crimson Corp assassin?"

His eyes widened in surprise, but my gaze narrowed on him, burned him with its accusation.

"You think *I* killed Jama."

"I think you're connected to him. I think you've got some pretty easy access to Crimson Corp, both their corporate building and their grounds, without being detected, caught, or questioned. I think you seem to know where I'll be even before I do. And I think Crimson Corp would do almost anything to keep the trail on Jama cold. Including putting on a little murder mystery theater. Giving us, *me*, false information and the runaround so that they can have *just* enough time to cover their tracks. The question now is, 'what happens when one of the detectives they've hired gets too close to the truth?'"

Aikan smiled, impressed. One of his hands was hidden—his fist clutching something under the folds of my bedsheets.

"That's a good question, Samira," he said. "What *does* one do with someone who's too close to the truth?"

I clenched my jaw, ready. I didn't have much strength to defend myself, but by God, I was going to die trying. "If you're planning to kill me—"

"You *protect* them."

As he said this, he looked at me, his eyes hard. He lifted his fist from the bedsheets, and in it, he held a key card. Spattered with blood, it dangled from a lanyard and had some rando's picture on it.

I blinked. "How'd you—"

"You asked what I was doing this entire time. I was cleaning up your tails."

"My—"

"Tails, yes. Sullivan had his goons tailing you, and I picked them off before they got too close. One was a scientist targeting you as a potential specimen. Luckily, I got to him first."

He tossed the key card into my lap. Clarence Martin. R&D department, Crimson Corp.

"He was going to be our way in to the truth. An *easy* way in. I tried to call you to tell you that, but of course, I hadn't expected you to bury your phone, or lose your mind and try to break *back* into Crimson Corp *alone*." He glared at me, and I shrank back. "I asked you to deliver the assassin if you caught him," he snarled. "Not to infiltrate Sullivan's company on a suicide mission."

"For all I know, with all your access to Crimson, you *are* the assassin!"

"Look at me, Samira. Smell me. Did I kill Jama? Did I kill Jama's wife?"

I leaned close to him, taking in the sultry scent of his skin. Bah. He was right. Werewolf, Arcane-hybrid, man, or not, I didn't smell his scent at any of the crime scenes. Just like Malcolm, Aikan wasn't the assassin. Didn't mean he was innocent ... but he wasn't a murderer.

"No," I said finally, relenting. "But it doesn't mean I trust you."

"That's okay. You're determined to take down Crimson Corp."

My nerves hardened. "Yes. I am."

"And there's nothing I can do to stop you."

"Not on your life."

"Good. Then, as I said, I'm coming with you."

"Yea—wait, *what?*"

"You want justice for the Jamas, and so do I. That makes us allies. I want Damon Sullivan and the man he hired to kill my friend to pay for their crimes."

Friend? I cocked my head and looked at him deeply, trying to read his face. Behind the hard exterior, the cocky alpha swagger, was a veil of pain. A fire, born from wounds too deep to speak of. He looked away and stood up.

"I put you on a drip of EverDark," he said. "It will take another 8 hours of dosing and rest to get you clear of the silver poison and the fevre. Only then will we go back to Crimson Corp. Together."

I furrowed my brow and did the math. "That puts me only about 6 hours out from the full moon. That's cutting it close."

"If you drop dead, you won't be cutting anything at all. Which one would you prefer?"

The answer was obvious. "I still don't trust you, Aikan. I still don't know anything about you, your connection to Jama, about this Ever-

Dark thing that all you Crimson cronies seem to be on. I need answers. Or I'm not going anywhere with you."

"If you live through the next 8 hours, I'll tell you everything you want to know." And with that, he walked out of the room, leaving me to my survival.

35

HISSING AT THE SKY

ALATHIA

My hands flew at the door handle, but it was too late. I was locked in. I smashed my palm up against the window and then kicked the door, even though I knew it was pointless. I'd had the Jag pimped out for extra security years ago after an attempted hijacking when I had the barrel of a black gun shoved into my face by some jerk at a traffic light. The windows were shatterproof. The tires were run-flat. The doors wouldn't flinch under machine gun fire, so the bite of my angry heels had little effect.

"Where's Edgar?" I demanded, reaching for my revolver. But they were too fast, and the passenger in the front seat magically whipped it out of my hand. I pictured poor Edgar tied up and gagged in the trunk, drunk on noxious fuel fumes. "Where is he?"

The driver took his time to answer, his attention mostly on the road and the steering wheel in his hands. "He's safe."

Their uniforms were charcoal, with silver badges: government issue. Or, rather, Cloud Conclave issue. These weren't your run-of-the-mill kidnappers. They were council officials. Sirela's minions. Holy shit. I felt for my holster. I knew it was empty, but my fingers sought it out anyway and pressed down on the smooth leather.

I didn't know what to do. Attacking the men would be seen as treason and have dire consequences. If they hadn't already decided on my execution that would seal the deal. I sat back against the seat, my mind spinning in 3-D. What did they know?

The silver-white scaled tower loomed before us, a giant albino snake hissing at the sky. We drove around and around in the parking basement, up and down, as if they were trying to throw off my sense of direction. They needn't have bothered. My reliance on Edgar's knowledge of the city meant I wouldn't know how to get to the nearest Crimson Deli drive-thru, never mind finding the correct entrance to Sirela's secret gold-leaf chamber. Something snapped on my hands—cold metal—and when I looked down, invisible handcuffs bound my wrists. One of the men—who looked like identical twins in their matching uniforms, crew cuts, and biceps—looked back at me and snapped his fingers, and a blindfold knotted itself tightly around my head.

I swore at them under my breath, using the dirtiest Croatian words I could think of. After we parked, the men pushed me in front of them and marched me into the building. I acted calm, even though my adrenaline was spiking and making my arms tingle. They guided me with sharp nudges and tugs. I hated the feeling of their skin on mine and the feeling that I was tipping forward, ready to stumble into the darkness that surrounded me.

It took around five minutes to reach our destination. It wasn't Sirela's chamber. There were no spiced cakes or peppermint tea, no freshly baked cinnamon buns. No perfume. This room smelled more masculine: a wood fire burning, coffee, warmed brandy. The minions scraped a chair across the room and forced me into it, pushing me down into an armchair scented with stale rum and maple smoke, which I supposed came from their pipes. No one smokes pipes anymore. No one but wizards. I had just been dragged before the nine-member Cloud Conclave, handcuffed and blindfolded. This wasn't going to end well.

"I won't be intimidated," I said. I wished my voice was firmer, but my nerves were grating my throat. "And if I find out you've hurt Edgar in any way I swear to—"

"Miss Laurent," said a mature male voice. He cleared his throat. "You've broken the cardinal rule."

Cardinal rule? Were they serious? There were murderers running riot and they decided to bring *me* in? "You've just kidnapped me," I replied. "Stolen my weapon and my driver. So ... *quid pro quo?*"

"You need to be punished," he said. "And making light of the situation will not further your cause."

"Look," I said. "I know I've been skirting the edges of what is legal—"

"You broke into the oldest and most prestigious club in the country!"

Calm down, old man, I wanted to say. *You'll give yourself a heart attack.*

Another wizard piped up. "And we all know that it's not your first offense."

"I don't know what kind of game you're playing," I said. "But you all know what my job is. You know I make the city a safer place."

They knew that Samira and I were responsible for getting more than our fair share of dangerous criminals off the streets. So why the brouhaha? And why was I using words like "brouhaha"? Their elitism was rubbing off on me.

"You think you're immune to the rules of the Dominion," said the old man. He was calm, but I heard the anger in his voice. I was a vampire —a woman, no less—and I wasn't kowtowing to the ancient code of conduct set out by our wizened forefathers.

Look, I wanted to say. *You do your job, and I'll do mine.*

But I bit my tongue (which is pretty painful if you're a vampire). I knew it wouldn't serve me to make the Conclave angrier than they were already. Even though it annoyed the hell out of me, I'd have to listen to what they had to say, then smooth talk my way out of there. I lifted my cuffed wrists and traced the edge of my blindfold with my fingers, formulating my thoughts.

"I want to protect the Masquerade as much as you do," I said. "If the Masquerade falls, my kind will be driven away. I'll no longer have a future here."

The old wizard slammed his staff on the floor in frustration. "Why then? Why be so brazen with the humans? Do you know they have footage of you?"

Except that vampires don't show up in photos or videos, so the Magnate Club security clip was as spooky as hell to watch, and would whip up a storm in the paranoid conspiracy theorist circles.

"Yes," I said. "I'm negotiating with the journalist to get the video deleted." There was an uncomfortable silence, so I added an extra few words, even if they stuck in my throat. "I'll do whatever I have to, to get rid of it."

"Miss Laurent. Do you know what happens to Arcanes who threaten the Masquerade?"

"Yes," I said. Prison; deportation if you were lucky. A sharp golden guillotine if you weren't.

"We've decided to give you one last chance."

Relief softened my body; my hands stopped perspiring. "Thank you."

"But to make certain you are taking this warning seriously," the old wizard said, "and to show that you cannot get away with breaking the law with impunity, you need a suitable punishment."

My head snapped up. "What?"

"You need to learn your lesson. For your sake and the sake of all the Arcanes."

"No," I said, shaking my head. "I've learned my lesson."

"May it be recorded in the book that Miss Alathia Laurent is to spend one hundred days in the internment camp."

One hundred days? What exactly was in those pipes they were smoking?

"No," I said, shaking my head. "I can't. I have a case to solve. A killer to catch. Don't you see that I'm *protecting* the Masquerade?"

"Take her away," said the wizard.

A white-hot hatred for the grandstanding old bastard surged through me.

"No!" I yelled, braced to fight back. But the two minions grabbed me and pushed me out of the room. About to punch the one on my left, a new voice arrived, calm and authoritative. I recognized it immediately; his voice and his scent. Despite my surprise, my muscles relaxed.

"Leave her to me," he said, and the rough men melted away. A firm hand—strong, but gentle—took my arm, and we walked out of the oppressive room together.

36

THE CRIMSON CONSPIRACY

SAMIRA

Eight hours and three naps later, I was still alive. Not only that, I felt so damned *good*! In fact, I was fully dressed, all yoga'd out, and bouncing around by the time Aikan had come back into the room. I guess he liked what he saw because as he looked me up and down, he beamed from ear to ear.

"See? Good as new," he said. "Let's go, the car's waiting."

I smirked at him devilishly. "Who needs a car?"

Evening was on us, and the approaching night felt good through my fur as I dashed through the wide open fields, gunning for the false mountains of Crimson Corp. Aikan's dirt bike tore up the earth next to me. Through his helmet, he gave me a wink as he revved up and then sped past me. Inside I smiled and kicked up my pace. Together we both raced into the sinking sun.

"So. You were going to spill the tea on, well, *everything*."

We'd stopped a mile off from the mountain. With our skills, it'd only be a five-minute jog from here. I had to get my clothes back on, so I'd started the conversation from behind a tree as I did.

Aikan sat with his back to the trunk, waiting for me.

"I was a prisoner of Crimson Corp for a long time," he said. "Jama was the one who set me free. It—I—was the reason he was murdered. He was my warden. By letting me go, he'd betrayed Crimson. He'd let a witness out into the world to reveal all their secrets. And for that, he was killed."

I stepped back around the tree, fully dressed. I crouched next to him and looked into his face. "I'm sorry," I said and meant it.

Aikan shrugged and looked off. "Shit happens, I guess."

"Why were you a prisoner of Crimson? What were they doing to you?"

In response, he lifted the EverDark capsule to my face. "*This* is what they were doing to me."

I blinked and looked at the EverDark more closely. I'd been on the stuff for the past two days and hadn't figured out what it was exactly. But Aikan looked like he was about to tell me.

"This is a genetic repressant designed specifically to repress the lupine genes in werewolves. Keeps you from transforming. But it also allows you to survive what would usually kill werewolves. Like silver."

"And it does so by making you 'less' werewolf?"

"Exactly. Crimson Corp manufactures this by the boatload. They are testing it on tons of Arcanes, and eventually, they'll use it to eliminate the werewolves altogether. Either by selling it to rival Arcanes like the vampires or the Nephilim ... or even by selling it to humans. *After* they've exposed the lupine sector of the Masquerade. Jama knew this, and his love for his girlfriend, and their kid, and for me as his friend, changed his tune on where he stood with Crimson. He helped me escape so that I could help take Crimson Corp down, and eliminate the EverDark plot for good."

My eyes widened, and I gripped my arms, terrified. "But why? Why do they want to get rid of *us*?"

"I have no idea. But I have a feeling that Crimson's in cahoots with some other entities. One of which is the group that the assassin belongs to. A group that I and some of my fellow escapees are trying to root out. The Scourge."

The Scourge. The EverDark plot. The Crimson conspiracy. It sounded like fodder for a pretty awesome novel. Totally unreal. Yet here we were. EverDark itself sat between us like some strange vessel of power with zero ethics. It could be a boon in the hands of good people, or evil in the hands of the wicked. I shivered as something occurred to me.

"You and Lila—you guys pumped that into me and never told me what it was doing?"

"Don't worry, pups. You'd need a way bigger dose over a much longer period in order for EverDark to ever have a permanent effect on you. Trust me, your body's already metabolized it by now. By the time the moon rises, you *will* transform."

"And what about you?" I leaned in closer. "You *are* a werewolf, aren't you?"

He set his jaw, his gaze suddenly very far away. "I was bitten by one a long time ago, and I managed to survive. I should have changed on the next full moon, but Crimson Corp found me before then. They took me in under the guise of wanting to 'help' me stay human. Tested EverDark on me, extensively. It worked. Mostly. I think. The full moon still makes me feel like shit, so ... I don't know *what* I am."

My face softened. "Well, maybe I can help you find out? Maybe, after we take down Crimson Corp, we can share the full moon together."

I had no idea know why these words leaped out of me, but they did, and in response, I slapped my hands over my mouth.

He looked at me and smiled. "Are you asking me out on a date?"

"No way!" I shook my head vigorously. "I was just—being friendly!"

"Sounded like you were asking me out on a date—"

"Oh, puh-*lease*—"

"I accept. But let's take down Crimson Corp first, eh?"

As I protested, he stood up and pulled me up with him. But he didn't let go of my shoulders. For a moment, we stood looking into each other's eyes.

I broke away, twiddling my fingers. "Ahem!" I cleared my throat and turned toward the road, toward the oncoming twilight. "Shall we?"

He pulled up next to me, pulling back the slide on his Glock 17. "Let's not keep Crimson Corp waiting."

37

A WIZARD'S BITE

ALATHIA

THE MAN LED me out of the Cloud Conclave chamber. His grip began to relax.

"Where are you taking me?"

"Just play along," he murmured into my ear.

I kept walking under his guidance until we were far away from the pipe smoke. We traveled up in an elevator and walked further to reach a door. I heard him unlock it. He pushed me inside, clicking open my handcuffs and pulling off my blindfold. The invisible cuffs went into his pocket.

The room was magnificent. It was the sky-gazing dome above the penthouse. The closest to the stars I'd ever been. And there he was, exactly as I remembered him. Dark-rimmed specs, Atlantic eyes, handsome face.

I felt a little out of breath. "Vane."

"Alathia," he said, leaning hard on the door, slamming it shut.

He stepped closer to me. My breathing grew shallower still. It wasn't the time to be thinking of his broad chest or his beautiful hands. Wasn't the time to be leaning into him, heart hammering. The warm scent of his skin was delicious, and my lips fell open, my fangs zinged.

He stepped away from me momentarily, to lock the door. "You'll be safe here."

The click of the bolt may as well have been the crack of a starting pistol. My body launched toward him. Surprise. Desire. I kissed him hard, and he returned my fervor. I pushed him up against the wall. My limbs were tingling with adrenaline and the longing for his body against mine. He took my shoulders and we spun, and then I was the one against the wall. His body pressed into me and pleasure zipped up my spine. A moan escaped my lips; as he increased his pressure, a louder one, more guttural. I wanted him immediately. Urgently. I reached for his belt, but he grabbed my wrist. He forced me to slow down, to enjoy the waves of longing pulsing through my liquid body, softening my knees, my lips, my brain. My mouth traveled to his neck. I couldn't help it. The skin there was soft and warm, and my fangs radiated with acute desire. It took everything I had not to bite him. He was unafraid, and his trust fortified my willpower. Instead, he ran his fingers through my hair, lighting up my scalp, and pulled my head to the side. His lips traveled to my throat and he bit my neck. Shocked, I exclaimed in pleasure, my whole body seizing with a deep ecstasy.

It was a human bite—a wizard's bite—but the thrill was immense, even though there would be no blood. My knees gave way and I collapsed; Vane caught me. He laid me down on the hardwood floor. I didn't mind the timber beneath me. I just cared about one thing, and that was having Vane consume me in every way. On his knees, he shook off his Conclave coat, putting it under my head as a makeshift pillow, and I pulled him down to kiss him again. Stars sparkled around us as if they were inside the sky-gazing dome with us. I noticed the discarded blindfold lying on the floor beside me and picked it up. I looked at

Vane, whose eyes burned in a mirror of mine. I gave him a playful smile and put the blindfold back on.

Afterward, we lay, fingers entwined, staring at the night sky. Thoroughly sated, my body hummed with pleasure. I didn't want to spoil the glow with words; nothing I could say would live up to the sheer physical joy of what had just happened. Instead, I tore my eyes away from the constellations and looked at him. Were all wizards this good in bed? Somehow, I doubted it. But having magic in their fingers was an advantage not to be underestimated.

I sighed loudly and stretched. Vane looked at me and ran his hand along my thigh.

"You," he said.

"Me?"

"I knew it would be this good."

I smiled and started pulling my clothes back on.

"From the second you walked into the room," he said.

He watched me dress and handed me my silver-tipped boots, which had only come off during the second round. He looked amused as I pulled them on.

"Aren't you going to say anything?" he teased.

I shrugged. "What is there to say?"

Of course, there was a lot to say. *Thank you for saving me from the internment camp. Thank you for risking your job for me. Thank you for the best shag I've had in centuries. And you're a Conclave wizard intern? Holy hex. You could have warned me.*

"I've got to go," I said.

"I'll walk you out. But, first, there's something I need to tell you."

I knew it was too good to be true.

"What is it?" I asked him, a tingle of fear creeping toward me like a flame.

"How well do you know your partner?"

I frowned. "What? Sami?"

"Do you trust her?"

"What are you talking about?"

Vane crossed his arms and started to say something, then stopped.

"What?" I demanded.

"Look. I'm not about to assume anything. But there are some things you need to know."

38

DEMONS IN THE DARK

SAMIRA

Aikan knew his way around Crimson Corp. Instead of going in through one of the many entrances, he took us around to the "dumping grounds."

"It's where Crimson Corp gets rid of its waste," he explained. "And not just Kota Joe wrappers. Chemicals, lab supplies, bodies."

I cringed at the thought that Crimson would consider bodies "waste," and more so that they were "dumped" rather than buried. The idea was grotesque. The more I learned about them and what they did to people, to *Aikan*, the more I hated them. The more I wanted to see them destroyed.

Without making a sound, we worked our way through the disposal system. A vile endeavor times 1000, considering that both of us had heightened senses of smell. We both struggled not to gag and only barely managed. Finally, though, we'd made our ways to a connecting lot resembling a parking port and sneaked into a side door that led into Crimson.

The level we stepped onto was one that few even knew existed. On it, he found a hidden freight elevator, one located in—surprise, surprise—

a bathroom. We cleaned ourselves up, liberally. I was grateful to find that he was just as much of a clean freak as I was. Then he swiped Martin's key card over a nearby tile.

I gasped in shock as the tiles moved in and slid to the side, revealing a titanium tube of sanitized metal. We squeezed in rather tightly, as the lift was really only made for one. The doors closed before we were lifted into the stars.

As Aikan shifted to give me more room, I became uncomfortably aware of how I could inhale his very essence in the small space. Strong, steady heartbeat, slow and calm breaths, that soap smell I was really starting to like. I made sure my eyes were turned into his chest, the only place I could look without feeling weird. But he didn't do me the same courtesy. He just stared at me, gently, greedily taking in with his eyes what he hadn't seen for days.

"Here's the mission," he started.

But his words are not words at all, but a whispery, soundless, and non-syllabic language I hadn't heard in years. Lupshin: a verbal communication developed by the first werewolves, and known naturally by all. Shocked, I finally looked him in the face.

"We get in," he said. "Grab samples, cultures, photos, evidence, and we get out. We go to the Cloud Concave and expose Crimson Corp so that Sirela can shut them down."

I set my jaw and nodded. I was ready to dropkick the world in the face at this point.

"There are dangerous things in the lab, Samira. Be careful."

His gaze anchored me as we continued to rise. The full moon was close, and my inner wolf had started to kick up. But looking at him calmed her down. Inside my chest, I could feel her nuzzle against his, like a newborn pup.

"Sami," I whisper in Lupshin.

"What?"

I smiled and bit my lip and finally tore my eyes away. "You can call me Sami."

The lift slid open, and I slipped out into the lab before he could say anything else.

The space was huge, a mad scientist's wet dream. The lab encompassed the entire top floor of Crimson Corp, which in total had to run at least a square mile in all directions. Divided into sectors and lab rooms, testing grounds, and data centers. I raised an eyebrow. No employees.

"Crimson's R&D division had a limited staff with special clearance. Jama was one of them, but his recent betrayal has Crimson Corp restructuring," his Lupshin whispers informed me. "Lab's officially shut down until they can tighten up their security protocols. It's a perfect opportunity. Let's not waste it."

I nodded, and we moved forward, getting down to business. As usual, I'd only brought my fists and blades with me, but Aikan had come prepared for espionage. He handed me medical gloves, a vial bag, and a compact camera, and we parted ways to gather evidence.

And boy was my trip enlightening. The room I'd found, *God*, was it a horror show. It alone would be enough to take Crimson down.

I walked in and clenched my stomach. Rows and rows of upright containment chambers, filled to the brim with convalescent fluid.

And bodies.

Dead, alive, sleeping. Arcanes of every ilk: vampires, Nephilim, wizards, magickals. Most were heavily sedated, kept alive only by the oxygen masks on their faces and the tubes that fed into their bodies. But mostly? There were werewolves. Sleeping, suspended and frozen in all different stages of transformation.

Unnatural. The Lupine Order needed the freedom to shift. It was against our genetic make-up to stay in one form forever. Crimson Corp was *damaging* these wolves. Destroying them.

I swallowed my anger and continued to take pictures, video, copies of notes and lab reports, anything I could get my hands on to take these bastards down.

I came upon an empty chamber. The only empty chamber. On the clipboard next to it, I could see the name: Aikan Salek. The notes on *that* board I took. If he wanted a cure to what Crimson had done to him, he'd need these. I folded them and stuck the papers into my vial bag.

After filling a single SD card and my vial bag with everything there, I walked a few minutes until I got to another lab. Along the way, I passed Aikan, who was rummaging through some scientists' desks in another room, getting all the tea. As I brushed by him, he nodded quietly. A gesture that meant "I'm watching you. Be careful."

I stepped into darkness and turned on the light. Woah. This lab was even bigger. And a *lot* more industrialized. Heavy, thick steel doors lined these walls, and behind them, creatures for which I had no name.

Because Arcane they were *not*.

Hungry and lethal-looking, these ... *things* were creatures not of this world, nor of any other world I knew. They were huge. Muscular and yet formless, with hellish deformed faces, impossibly serrated limbs broken and re-sewn together with what looked like glittering black threads of abyss. Thick armored plates shifted to protect various internal organs, like a skin that crawled on its own. Claws and teeth sharpened to a razor's edge, some with a canine influence and others with a vampiric one. Demons in the dark.

Almost immediately, the wolf in me whined and recoiled. Not even *she* wanted to be here, and that was an instinct I began to follow—until one of them trained its pupiless eyes on me... and *slammed* into the glass of its cell.

The glass spider-webbed, and a robotic voice announced, "EverDark specimen 5829 cell breached. Lab security lockdown commencing."

A bolt of fear struck my body. I turned and ran back toward the entrance.

"AIKAN!"

But my scream was cut off as a thick steel door slammed down in front of my only exit, trapping me. A Plexiglas panel in the door was the sole window into the hallway, and in the next second, Aikan's panicked face blinked into view.

Another *crack* behind me. Then a low hissing growl.

"AIKAN! OPEN THE DOOR!"

I slammed my fists into the steel. I even went wolf for a second and tried to claw my way through. No dice. Aikan desperately tried to break through the door himself and wrestled with the panel. It still wouldn't budge.

"SAMI! RUN! GO *NOW!*"

"But where?!"

Another *crack*, sharper this time. Something had given way in the creature's cell. To my left, more steel doors had started coming down in the middle of the room. From the *ceiling*. Which meant ...

I didn't think. I ran. I slid under the descending steel doors and rolled back into a sprint. If these doors were coming down, it meant there was a part of the lab that was vulnerable. *Escapeable*. I just had to get to it before—

SMASH!

Behind me, the unmistakable sound of hell unleashed. So too was my adrenaline as I ran ever faster, clearing obstacles: chairs, tables, lab gurneys. Endless rows of steel rolled down to the ground, tightening my maneuverable space.

I pumped my arms, tearing my way through the labs and toward the only way out that I could see, the large row of windows up ahead.

Plexiglas, it's Plexiglas, you WON'T get through it.

I wouldn't. But the wolf would. I leaped over a long table in front of me, transforming as I did. My furry head grazed the steel door that was now only five feet off the ground. I hit the linoleum on all four paws and broke the air around me as I took off across the lab.

The demon was almost on me.

Tables and chairs flew into the ceilings, walls, and the ever-approaching steel doors as the EverDark demon ripped through the space behind me, hunting me, opening its jaws to devour me.

Its teeth close on my tail tip, I jumped, crashing through the thick glass of the lab and into the night.

The 100-foot fall would have killed anyone but a Lycana.

Right before I hit the ground, I went human again. I landed hard and rolled. And rolled. And rolled some more. The inertia was running its course, but I was fine, and the bruises that had spread over my body from the landing were already healing as I rolled to my feet and kept running.

The loud screech of tires and the screams of sirens finally stopped me. I skidded and raised my hands as my body became awash in a bright hot spotlight. Terrified more of what was behind me than what was in front of me, I looked over my shoulder at the window I'd just come through.

Nothing. For whatever reason, the demon hadn't followed, but I *could* see its viscous limbs clinging to the inside of the lab window. Watching.

The screaming men in front of me, though, didn't notice. They couldn't see like I could. They only saw me.

"Put your hands in the air and get on your knees! NOW!" The commanding voice boomed through a megaphone. "You are under arrest."

39

BLOOD MOON

ALATHIA

"That murder weapon," said Vane. "The X-Blades. They were stolen from the Museum of Magical History."

"I know that."

"My contact there had a forensic team investigate the theft. The conclusion was that a werewolf had switched the artifact for the fake."

"A werewolf stole the X-Blades?"

"There was evidence of a wolf. Minuscule traces. I said I'd do what I could from this side to find out who it could be. Then I find out your partner is a Lycana."

I wanted to laugh. Was he seriously saying what I thought he was saying? Samira was no thief.

"Her records show she's in debt, which would account for motive."

"Samira's always in debt," I said. "But she's never stolen anything in her life."

"There are other things that point to her."

"Like what?"

"The museum is in New York City."

I knew Samira was innocent, but I could agree the evidence looked pretty damning. "What else?"

"It would explain how Benedict Jama got pinned to your pretty wallpaper. No one else has access to your office, right?"

"Right," I said. Of course, I didn't think Samira was the killer, but she had been acting super cagey lately. I was positive she was hiding things from me, even lying, which was not like her at all. Was someone forcing her to play a game I didn't know about?

"Look," Vane said. "I'm not going to take any of this to the Conclave. Not yet. Not until I know more. I just thought you should know."

I stared at him. "Thank you."

There was an awkward silence. My phone rang. I grabbed for it, hoping it was Sami.

"Laurent," said a gruff-sounding Malcolm. I didn't know why he called me by my surname, but I preferred it over "vampire lady," which he had called me before.

"You need to get down here," he said. "Now."

I scanned the room, making sure I hadn't left anything behind. Only the blindfold lay on the floor. Vane reached into his wizard cloak and pulled out my revolver. He handed it to me. Our skin sparked when we touched. I looked into his eyes as I returned the gun to its holster.

Speaking into my phone, I asked, "Where?"

"Sandton police station," he said. "They've got her."

"What?"

"Samira," he said. "They've got her."

Adrenaline mainlined my bloodstream. He was a rambling madman. He was paranoid. He jumped to conclusions. I tried not to allow his fear to infect me. There had to be a reasonable explanation. I looked up through the glass dome, noticing for the first time how full and red the moon looked.

It was a blood moon. I had a very bad feeling.

40

A CHORUS OF SCREAMS AND BLOOD

SAMIRA

I WANTED to tell Alla and Malcolm what I'd seen. About the secret torture lab underneath Crimson Corp. About Arcanes I'd never seen before. New, dangerous Arcanes that even the Cloud Concave and Sirela would hold meetings to hear about. About EverDark. Where it had come from ... and what Sullivan planned to do with it.

But that bastard Sullivan had already made sure I'd never open my mouth to anyone. And it was my fault that he'd succeeded.

The police dragged me into the station, and for fear of hurting them, I didn't fight. They were innocent. Human. Called by Crimson's built-in security system. They knew nothing about the Masquerade, or Sullivan, or anything, and they shouldn't have to die because of it.

Despite all my efforts, they still just might.

By the time the police printed me, mugshot me, processed me, and threw me into my cell, I was breathing hard, sweating, and pacing. An hour away from my transformation, and my body was already roiling. Itchy skin, bloodshot blurry eyes, a mouth as dry as the ass of a sand snake. The wolf was taking over, my human self withering away in the process. What the silver fevre had done to me earlier would be nothing compared to what the blood moon was about to do.

Supernova plus a big-ass nuke. That was always the image that came to mind on these nights. A supernova and a nuclear warhead, both going off inside a human body at the same time, giving birth to a horrible, bloodthirsty, and all-powerful wolf creature. An abomination that would crawl from the radioactive post-apocalypse ooze that would become my body's ground zero. And then ... everyone would die. In a chorus of screams and blood.

Yeah.

Dramatic, I know. But exactly what was about to happen if I didn't get out of there. I *needed* to get out of there ... or everyone in the Sandton police station would die.

"LET ME OUT! PLEASE! LET ME OUT, I DON'T WANT TO HURT ANYONE!"

I grabbed the bars of my cell, reared back, and screamed. Long and loud. But even *I* heard the wolf's howl inside the shrill human voice. The metal bars shrank beneath the growing strength of my grip. And my skin itching as hair follicles worked overtime. And the hunger, the lust for blood, spiking in my diaphragm.

I could feel it all. I could feel the wolf wake up.

41

PUG IN A PINK COLLAR

ALATHIA

I TORE down the emergency stairwell. Vane yelled after me. He wanted to know where I was going, wanted to come with me, but I didn't have time for that. I needed to break Sami out of that police station before she transformed and hurt innocent people. Before she was killed. I flew down the tower, not caring which doors I smashed or who saw me do it. I didn't know where my car was, or where Edgar was. I'd have to make my way to the police station. As I stood on the pavement, the tower shimmering behind me, a beat-up old sedan rumbled toward me. The panels were mismatched and dented, held together with rust, old paint, and a bad welding job. Black smoke streamed from the perforated exhaust pipe. The windshield was grimy and spider-webbed with a large crack. Despite my rush, I had to stop and stare at it as it slowed to a stop in front of me.

"Hey!" shouted Malcolm, turning to look at me while he gripped the steering wheel like a grinning madman. The car heaved, choked, spluttered ... and generally threatened to die. I stared at it, and again at Malcolm.

"Well?" he said. "What are you waiting for?"

. . .

Reluctantly, I climbed in, and Malcolm told me what he knew. A pug in a pink collar panted in the back seat.

"That's Rosie," he said.

I looked at the dog. "Hi, Rosie."

He jammed his foot down on the accelerator, and we were on our way, the car lurching and belching. According to Malcolm, while I was "gallivanting with wizards" (his words), Samira had broken into Crimson Corp and unleashed all hell.

"I wasn't gallivanting," I retorted. "I was kidnapped."

He raised his eyebrows and looked pointedly at the bite mark on my neck. Annoyed, I shifted my collar to hide the bruise.

"How did you know I was here, anyway?"

Was he really a non-magical human? He seemed to know a lot for someone on his side of the Masquerade. Did he have supernatural ability?

"The same way I know where Samira Shaw is," he said. He brought out an old, cracked tablet. It was in a heavy-duty case, like something you'd have in a warzone. He showed me the screen, which happened to match his car's front window. A blue icon radiating animated waves indicated a tracking device at the police station.

"Bastard! You put a tracker on her?" Then I punched him. "You put a tracker on me?"

He looked satisfied with himself. "They're so evolved nowadays. You can pretty much put a tracker on anything."

I glared at him.

"For your safety," he added, then quickly stowed the tablet away.

Ugh. "Can this thing go any faster?"

"Sure," he said, grinning. "I'll just engage the turbo blaster."

A block from the police station, Malcolm's junker finally gave up the ghost. With one last brave heave and then a pitiful whimper, the car rolled to a painfully slow stop. Malcolm grabbed his stuff, hoisted Rosie to his chest, and balanced her on his arm. She yapped.

We jogged the last mile, and arrived at the cop shop out of breath, looking like a post-apocalyptic rag-tag couple on the lam. It wasn't the most discreet entrance I'd ever made, but I didn't care. Malcolm tried to keep up. I mesmerized anyone who stood in my way. I didn't care about guns or cameras; all I cared about was getting to Samira's cell. I was seconds away.

I had to break her out before she turned full wolf or innocent people would die. Sami would die. And the Masquerade would be nothing but a memory.

42

BACK

SAMIRA

THE MUSCLES IN MY LEGS, arms, and back swelled. My bones stretched, giving me height, changing my face. Dark, black hair sprouted from every follicle.

"Please ..." I begged myself softly. "Please just wait ..."

But the she-wolf would not "wait." I was only a few more minutes out from the full moon, and there was no stopping it. The wolf was fully awake and mauling the cage in my mind. Hands I could no longer control wrapped around the cell bars and pulled, ripping them from their cement mounts.

The world before me collapsed in a riot of debris, torn metal, and smoke. Somewhere deep in my human brain, I heard the screams of my cellmates.

They sounded like fresh meat. Fat, juicy, ambulating steaks marinating in fear and adrenaline. I stepped out of my cell and into the hallway. I sniffed and closed my eyes. My senses dialed up a thousand-fold, and in my mind's eye, I visualized and smelled the entire police station. Fleshies were on their way, drawn by the screams.

Hungry.

The wolf wanted to run *toward* the screams of terror, toward the approaching cops, but I fought her, pushed her to go the opposite direction. My stomach growled, and drool slipped out of my open jaw as the wolf's mind wrapped around mine. Suffocating it.

As what was left of me dissipated under the weight of the Wolf, my body turning, walking toward the shrill screams—

"SAMI!"

Another scream, this time familiar, cut through the others and drew the wolf's gaze. The wolf turned around, and for a moment, human me breathed and saw.

"A-*Alla?*"

But I was silenced as the wolf took over again and licked its jaws. Through its eyes, I saw Alla's face fill with terror. Then she spun around and hightailed it.

Howling, the wolf tore down the hallway after her.

dn't

I didn't care where the vampire lady was leading me. All I cared about was feeling her body crunch between my teeth. She made a sharp turn around a corner. But I was too big, too fast, still transforming—and crashed into the wall that had rushed up to meet me. I stood up and shook off the stars. I heard the pitter-patter of feet, her feet, trying desperately to put distance between us.

As if.

I leaped, chasing the sounds down and halving the distance in seconds. I slid into a room, and despite the fact that it was drenched in darkness, I saw the scattered desks, the paper clutter, the old equipment. A storage room. She wasn't here, but she'd been through here. I smelled her sweat, her panic, her delicious terror. I jumped again, making it across the room in a single bound, and when I landed, the floor tiles crunched under my feet.

I followed the vamp's footsteps into the next room—and light sliced into the darkness as a back exit door swung open. The wind from outside blew in—and her silhouette escaped into the night.

I morphed into quadruped form and launched myself toward the door, bursting into the night. My vision sharpened on the vamp's thin, munchable frame. I jumped. The vamp hit the deck.

BAM!

A shot thundered through the night, and a sudden force tore into my left shoulder, knocking me off course. I tumbled and yipped, as a dart drove deep into my body.

When I tried to get up, I found that it was nearly impossible. My body was still massive, but somehow, my strength had been sapped by half. I looked up to see the face of my assailant.

A half-wolf man. He held a rifle, aimed it. At *me.*

I slowly rose to all fours. My paw closed around the dart in my shoulder and yanked it out. Snarling, I threw it to the ground and focused my hunter's glare on the man who'd just signed his death warrant.

Not a man. A combination of man and werewolf. A half-breed. Were-wolf or not, I intended to tear off his head.

I kicked up large clumps of concrete as I charged.

Half-wolf didn't move. Instead, he pulled the rod back on the tranq rifle and loaded another dart, calm. I'd change that. I'd rip off that stupid half-wolf's face and hear him scream and—

The next dart hit me in the neck. And *this* time, whatever was in it worked, because I couldn't get up. I shuddered as sudden ice rushed through my veins, drowning the wolf.

"SAMI!" The vamp screamed my name for a second time, and crouched beside me.

My swollen muscles atrophied, my fur receded, and my bones liquefied and re-calcified into their human structure. My body deflated, shrinking, changing—until I was a normal girl again.

I was back.

43

SILVER BULLETS

ALATHIA

THERE WAS no time to talk. There was no time to do anything but heft an unconscious Sami over my shoulder and evacuate the police station, still smoking with cement dust and bent metal. The strange male introduced himself as "Aikan" and moved to take her from me. I hissed at him. Sure, he'd just saved Sami's life, and my life, and all the muggles in the station, but there was no way I'd let him take my best friend's insensate body anywhere.

"Back off, wolverine," I warned, showing him my fangs.

Aikan didn't back down. He stepped forward, towering over me. "Samira is one of us," he said. "She belongs with her people."

He tried to take her from me, and my hand automatically unclipped my revolver. The cool ivory grip felt good in my hands. I brought it up and aimed it squarely at Aikan's face, releasing the safety catch as I did so.

"Silver bullets," I said.

"Fine." he backed away with his hands in the air. "But let us work together."

Malcolm's eyes widened, and his cheeks bloomed pink. He stood, speechless, gripping Rosie, who barked her head off. It was as if all his Arcane conspiracy theories had come true in one night, and he didn't know what to do with himself.

Samira stirred, and a low moan escaped her lips.

"We need to go," I said, and they both nodded.

"Alla," she whispered.

"Ssshh," I said. "You're okay."

"She's not okay," insisted Aikan, and I had an urgent need to punch him. "None of us are *okay*. If we don't stop Sullivan tonight, it'll be over for us. The wolves, the vampires. Everyone."

Sami groaned again and put her palm on her forehead, close to surfacing. The dazed humans would seek us out soon.

Where would Damon Sullivan be late on a Friday night?

44

BECAUSE WE WEREWOLVES ARE LIKE THAT

SAMIRA

Aside from hunger, the first thing I felt when I woke up was annoyance. This was the third time I'd passed out in three days, and it was pretty embarrassing. Especially because every time I woke up, someone was looking squarely into my face with his or her wide buggy eyes.

This time was no different, except I had the honor of getting a two-for-one special. Both Alla *and* Aikan were looking me in the face when my eyes fluttered open.

"ARGH!! JEEZ!" I screamed and crabbed back reflexively. "You guys are weirdos, you know that?"

Aikan was smiling, and Alla was … frown-smiling? I dunno. I could never tell with her. But she wrapped her arms around my neck and hugged me tight. Woah. Whatever happened must've been super serious, because the woman was *not* a huggy person.

She separated from me, cold fury in her face. "You worried the shit out of me."

I scratched my head, genuinely confused. "I'm … sorry? But what happened? What did I do?"

She looked at me, bewildered. "WHAT IN THE ENTIRE NINE CIRCLES OF HELL DO YOU MEAN 'WHAT HAPPENED'?!" she exploded, and I held up my hands to shield myself from her wrath.

Aikan stepped in. "A werewolf's short-term memory is pretty terrible around the full moon, Alathia," he explained to her. "You probably wouldn't know because Sami stays away from you this time of the month. But hold on."

From the foot of the bed, he pulled out a wad of fabric and held it under my nose. My clothes from the past three days. One whiff gave me a sensory story of the past 72 hours, and immediately, it all came back to me. The Wolfsbane, Lila the other werewoman, the assassin at the Jamas's, the trek through Crimson Corp, the EverDark demon, YES.

"OH YEAH!" I piped up. "Alla! I have *so* much to tell you."

All the details came out: about Crimson Corp and its secret torture dungeon, about the new Arcanes, about how Sullivan was a totally bogus bitch and how we needed to kick his ass and bring him down, and—but Alla held up her hand and stopped me mid-sentence. All the new intel notwithstanding, she looked upset. With *me*.

"Are you going to explain how you met *him*?"

She indicated Aikan, stationed coolly in the corner, watching the entire exchange without saying a word. This time, though, he swayed to a stand. "I'll be outside."

After the door closed behind him, I took a deep breath and sighed. "I've been working with Aikan from the beginning ..."

"And?"

"He said that he has info on my family and will give it up if I bring Jamas's assassin to him instead of the police."

Alla's eyes narrowed. "*And?*"

"Aannd he's part of a secret Arcane freedom fighting group that is trying to take down Crimson Corp and another dark cabal before they destroy the world?"

Alla's eyes flickered. Maybe with hurt. Shamefaced, I continued, telling her about how I was so desperate to see my family that I was willing to risk everything, even our friendship, to get closer to them. About how I felt ashamed and sorry for lying to her. How I desperately needed her to forgive me.

Then I started bawling. Because, you know, we werewolves are like that.

A long silence passed, and Alla stared at me with those hard, unforgiving eyes of hers. Finally, she said: "I slept with the wizard."

"HUH?!" I sniffed and laughed as I rubbed my wet eyes. "Wait ... *what* wizard?"

She smiled at me slyly. "Exactly." She put a comforting hand on my shoulder. "Everyone has secrets, Sami. Things we want that we have to pursue alone. I get it. I understand that better than most. Just ... next time a secret of yours is liable to get us killed, maybe tell me about it?"

I sniffled again and nodded. "Okay. The truth. Well ..." I took a deep breath and then let loose. "I would like to go kick everyone's ass at Crimson Corp, and it's probably going to get us killed. And I'd also like to invite along a group of werewolf chicks who hate Crimson Corp and want to bring it down too. And they also might kill us. And Aikan's team might also kill us. Everyone might kill us. There."

Alla laughed. A sound rarely heard in our world, but it brought sunshine to my heart. She looked at me and nodded. "Great. Thank you for that. Now, let's go kick some Crimson ass."

45

FROZEN FIRE

ALATHIA

WE RAN OUTSIDE to the road bathed in marmalade streetlight, looking like a gang of extras from *Mad Max* meets *An American Werewolf in Paris*. Rosie was still yapping, so I gave her a look that would freeze fire, and she stopped. One more sharp little bark and she'd get one of Aikan's tranq darts in a main artery.

Outside on the road, we had no way to get to the Magnate Club, and we could hardly call an Uber. I mean, no one would pick us up looking the way we did. Helpless wasn't a feeling I was used to.

Out of the corner of my eye, I saw a dark vehicle on the horizon zooming toward us. It couldn't be. Could it? This rescue vehicle couldn't be more different from Malcolm's pile of rusted junk. It was dark, sleek, and a beauty to behold.

"Edgar!" I yelled, letting my excitement get the better of me. We piled in and slammed the door shut. I felt safe for the first time in hours.

"I thought they'd locked you up somewhere," I said. "I thought—"

"There's nothing to worry about," said Edgar. "I can assure you that I'm perfectly fine."

But my sleuth's eye told a different story. His suit was slightly wrinkled—Edgar has never worn a wrinkled suit in his life—and he had a large purple bruise on the back of his hand. He had fought to escape. He had fought to find me. I swallowed hard.

"Where would you like me to take you this evening?"

It was a full moon. Without hesitation, I said, "The Magnate Club."

Everyone in the car turned to look at me.

"Are you sure?' Aikan said.

"No," I said. "But it's my best guess."

Aikan looked annoyed and he flared his nostrils, as if he thought my best guess wasn't good enough.

I squared my shoulders. "Unless Aikan has a better idea?"

He looked out of the window, the muscles in his strong jaw working.

"I don't know what you see in him," I said to Sami. She rolled her eyes in solidarity.

Edgar didn't wait for a unanimous vote. I was his boss, so he put his foot down, easing the car into a good solid purr. Rosie looked at me, as if mesmerized.

I'm sorry, I said telepathically. *I didn't mean the part where I said I'd dart you.*

I don't know if she understood English, but she seemed to relax against Malcolm's chest.

"You'll want to leave Rosie in the car for this next bit," I said.

Malcolm nodded and pulled her tighter toward him, kissing her on the head.

. . .

At the Magnate Club, I remembered thier pimped out their security system, shook my head, and swore under my breath in Croatian. It looked even more militarized now. It looked like a goddamn citadel.

"What the what?" said Samira, peering out at the men in uniforms with AK-47s. They wore night-vision goggles, the ones that protect humans from mesmerizing vampires.

"It's my fault," I said. "They've doubled up on security since my last ... visit."

Malcolm smirked, presumably because of my choice of words. I shot him a visual dagger.

Edgar kept cruising, and we went around the back of the old building. I cast a glance over at Sami. She looked stronger, but had trauma written all over her body.

"You ready for this?" I asked.

She nodded, yellow flames flickering in her eyes.

Rosie didn't yap.

46

SOME INCEL SHIT

SAMIRA

THE PLAN: my Lycana friends would clear the way for Alla and Malcolm inside the club. Aikan and I were going to lay some bodies out in the yard. But of course, Aikan spent more time flirting than he did skulking.

As we snuck through the gardens, Aikan whispered to me for a second time. "Smart friend you've got there," he said with a smirk. "Didn't know that the 'walking in the front door' approach was so furtive and inconspicuous."

He was talking about Alla. I rolled my eyes. Again.

"Didn't hear *you* coming up with any mind-blowing ideas," I muttered.

"Sorry, guess I was distracted by your ethereal beauty and come hither scowl."

"Ugh."

I crouched, hearing the movements of a patrolling guard. He crouched with me, but faced the opposite direction. Guards, unbeknownst to them, flanked us from behind. We stared into our respective distances, homing in on our targets at the same time.

Suddenly, he chuckled. "How about a race?"

The guards were getting closer, but I speared a sharp look over my shoulder and hissed. "*What?!*"

"I go my way and you go yours, and whoever takes out all their guards and gets back here first wins."

"We're on a mission, that's freaking ridicul—"

"One, two, GO!"

And he was off, having taken out his first guard and tearing through the greenery like a silent, deadly wind. I groaned, but my inner wolf was game for the competition. She *hated* to lose.

So I sprang forward, and my wolf and I became one as we silently made our rounds through the lush conservatory. One guard, two guards, three guards, four ... I took all of them out with grace, style, and speed, and like Aikan, I didn't make a sound. When I'd finished my circuit, my side of the gardens was cleaned out. Unconscious bodies littered the ground like man-sized breadcrumbs, gingerbread men, really, with fat blue knots baked into their heads.

My cheeks were flushed, and my blood was hot. Smiling, I jogged back to our starting point—until I stopped short and frowned. Aikan lay relaxing under a tree. He grinned as he played a game on his cellphone. He'd been waiting here a while.

Without looking up, he smirked. "What took you so long, pups? I've had time to bake a cake and eat it while you've been away."

I huffed. That was total BS. I'd only taken a couple of minutes, for crying out loud. "Whatever. It's not like there's a prize."

"Says who?" And this time he looked up at me, still smiling. "It's not your game, it's mine. And my prize is that date you offered earlier."

"WHAT? How are you going to award *yourself* a date with me? That's some incel shit if I've ever heard it!"

"Why not? I like you. You *clearly* like me."

My face was on fire. This was hardly the time to discuss the status of our non-existent relationship. "Boy, bye! Get over yourself!"

"I mean, what's the problem? Are you and Alla ...?"

And by his shit-eating grin, I could tell what he was implying. Was he freaking serious?!

He smirked and stood up. "Well, consider *my* heart broken. Ah well. We'd better get back to your girlfriend."

"SHE'S NOT MY GIRLFRIEND!" I snapped. "We're just friends, and you and I are *not* dating, and now we are going to break into a club and kill people! So, if you'll EXCUSE me ..."

I brushed by him, annoyed. Alla was totally right about this ham-headed, blow-hard son-of-a ... Argh. Still, the warmth on my back came from his smile, and for whatever reason, I was happy to have it.

Hopefully, with what we were doing tonight, it wouldn't be the last time I'd get to see it.

47

WHOREWOLF PIRATES

ALATHIA

With the security breached by Samira and her new friends—the band of whorewolf pirates—Malcolm and I were able to creep into the back entrance of the Magnate Club. Sami joined us, out of breath. I brushed a leaf off her shoulder and gestured to the wolves prowling the perimeter.

"What are they doing here?" I whispered to Sami.

"I told them we'd be needing their help," she said.

"Since when are werewolves so eager to help someone not in their pack?"

"They're not here for us. They're here for them." She gestured toward the interior of the club. From what I could tell, some of the men inside had abused Lycana, so this would be sweet justice.

"I love it when a plan comes together," Malcolm said, and Rosie yapped.

"Jesus, Malcolm, I told you to leave the hound in the car."

. . .

We made it past the guards, who were being held to the ground by the vicious jaws of the wolf pack. But as we stepped inside, something changed. There must have been an invisible tripwire, and we'd walked right into it. The heavy metal door we'd just strode through slammed shut, as did the one in front of us, and a siren began to wail.

"That'll alert the cops," said Malcolm.

"You're not helping," I snapped at him. Things had been going well for a full two minutes before we had managed to lock ourselves in this solid metal cage. I gnashed my teeth in frustration. Damn it!

The siren grated my brain, corroding my thoughts till I was no longer able to think straight. I slammed my hand against the door keeping us out of the club.

"I can't go back to a jail cell," said Samira.

"You're not going back to a jail cell," I said. No way would let that happen. But if I didn't think of something fast, that's exactly where we'd all end up. Frustrated, I hit the door again, and there was a heavy clunking sound.

I stepped back. Uh-oh. Now what had I done?

The door was unlocking itself. What was this sorcery? But then it opened all the way, revealing the majestic downstairs reception area, where, on the expensive oriental carpet stood not an elf, but a wizard.

He held his Magnate employee access card and looked pleased with himself.

"Welcome," said Vane, with a sweep of his arm.

With all the chaos and craziness, I had almost forgotten that he worked here. Despite the circumstances, I broke into a wide grin. How often does it happen that a seriously good-looking wizard saves your vamp bacon twice in one day?

"I've been expecting you," he said. He led us to the secret staircase. "Your timing couldn't have been better. They're all here," he said. "In one room."

We bounded down the stairs, all five of us. Once the wolves had finished with the guards outside, they'd join us, too. I expected guards at the door of the opulent dining room; I expected to have to hijack a catering tray and uniforms to be able to get in, but these people were laid bare by their arrogance. Yes, the entrance to the room was guarded, but Vane knew the old building like a D&D player knows a Turtle Dragon map. He led us to the kitchen, where we crept in. Proper stealth mode activated, we flattened ourselves against the steamy walls. We dealt quickly and quietly with any waiters or kitchen staff who came our way. I mesmerized those I could, and Vane had a nifty freezing spell that he used on the staff who wouldn't look me in the eyes. Together we made our way through the massive kitchen. Dishwashers stood frozen, hands still in the soapy water, soup-stirrers dropped their ladles with a clang. The food being prepared was no ordinary dinner. We walked past trays of dozens of oysters, shrimp cocktails, and salmon ceviche with cracked black pepper. There were golden roast chickens, buttery potatoes, caramelized carrots. Ostrich fillet wrapped in herbs and flaky pastry. Bright red lobsters, peri-peri prawns, and deep-fried soft-shell crabs. I couldn't tell for sure, but it looked as if they were celebrating something. Samira was too, apparently, as she plucked a sample from every tray we passed by. We arrived at the serving door. Vane put his shoulder to the door and pulled his wand from his robe.

"Ready?" he whispered.

I looked at Sami, and she nodded, swallowing her last shrimp. The wolf in her, the animal instinct radiated off her in hot waves. I felt it and smelled it as the animal in her met the animal in me. I turned back to Vane and unclipped my revolver.

"Ready," I said.

Vane short-circuited the access panel with a potent electric spell, then used brute force to smash the door open. We rushed into the opulent dining room, Malcolm brandishing pink-collared Rosie like a weapon. No one noticed us at first, so occupied were they with their respective conversations and their gourmet food. It gave me time to scan the room. I saw wizards of all creeds, witches, vampires, and the occasional troll. What caught my attention was the huge table that was set out, looking as if it was set for a royal family. Swathed in expensive fabrics, it bristled with golden cutlery and goblets. The chairs were empty, set to have the mother of all celebratory parties, but the royalty had not yet arrived. The guests looked up and shouted for the guards. Little did they know Samira's new best friends, the Lycana from Wolfsbane, had taken care of the security force.

As if summoned, those wolves entered the hall, too, and they looked ready to kill. Crushing teeth bared, blood on their lips. The sight made my fangs zing in anticipation. A man in a tuxedo approached me. I hissed at him and struck him in the chest. My adrenaline-laced vampire strength was no match for him; he fell backward, splayed on the floor.

I looked around, ready for the next attacker. Malcolm had gone full-on Rambo, shouting and jumping on people, taking them down and zip-tying their wrists while Rosie danced on the royal table, eating roast chicken off china plates and drinking water out of the glittering goblets. Samira took on a vampire as if it were the bad old days, ready to tear him limb from limb. But the man wised up and ran for it.

I spotted Damon Sullivan trying to escape.

"Stop him!" I yelled, pointing my gun at his chest. He was almost out of the door. I gave him one last warning. "Sullivan!" I shouted.

I looked around, hoping someone from my team would tackle him, but they were all busy defending themselves. Nobody to stop Sullivan but me. I didn't want to kill him, though. I had too many questions.

I gave him one last warning. "Sullivan!" I shouted. I glanced down at the table and grabbed the carving knife and fork set. He paused for a split second, looking at me. It felt like we were moving in slow motion. I took careful aim and threw them as hard as I could, and they flew like metal darts across the room, pinning Sullivan to the wall. It was sweet justice for Jama ... but Sullivan was still alive and kicking. I blurred toward him and hissed, my fangs sharp against my lips.

Sullivan struggled against his luxurious business suit, trying to escape.

"You utter bastard," I spat, my face contorting in anger and revulsion. "You're an evil excuse for a human." I jammed my revolver into his chest. "You're a piece of shit, Damon Sullivan. Give me one reason not to send this silver bullet into your frozen heart right now."

Sullivan slowed his struggles, his body shaking.

"Let me go," he uttered. "Please. Let me go."

"Let you *go?*"

"Please," he said, his chin trembling.

"You didn't let Samira go. You didn't let the others go."

"You don't understand," said Sullivan. "It was never us. It was never me."

"You're such a coward!" I shouted. "Trying to shift the blame now that you've been caught."

"I promise you," he said. "I swear on my life. They forced us to develop and implement EverDark. We all had to cooperate or die."

"Who?" I asked, but he shook his head, too afraid to answer. I helped him along by crushing his junk in the palm of my hand. He screamed in an appropriate manner.

"Tell me!" I said.

It took him a second to regain his composure. He licked the sweat off his lips and said, "Don't you think it's odd that the Cloud Conclave never investigated the Crimson Corp ?"

I blinked at him. Hadn't it? It sure had enough complainants. Sullivan had given us a whole list of them. Had he been trying to tell us something? I thought he was trying to throw us off the scent, but maybe it was a double-cross. He had given us Malcolm. Was that also on purpose? To help steer us toward the truth?

Whether or not he'd been trying to harm us or help us, he was correct. I'd never heard of the Nine Cloud Conclave doing an audit on Crimson Corp.

"We have access to unlimited capital for new product development. We've never had to have our new products approved by any regulatory body."

"What are you saying?" I asked, narrowing my eyes at him and squeezing harder.

He yelped. "You know what I'm saying. The answer is right in front of you." His eyes stole over to the royal table, which was still empty, aside from a panting pug.

I remembered the harsh treatment I'd received at the hands of the Conclave heavies. The hundred-day sentence they'd so easily handed out to me without a trial. Sullivan's eyes were wide and clear. "They wanted you and your werewolf girlfriend out of the picture so that they could push EverDark into the market. They wanted werewolves gone for good. EverDark will wipe out the Lycana, and for the trouble-makers—the people who get in the way—they brought in the Scourge assassin."

"The Scourge?"

I had heard rumors of the Scourge before; had never known if they were true. They were Arcane hunters. Part mercenaries, part religious freaks; their mission was to eliminate every supernatural being in the Dominion.

"The Scourge assassin killed Benny Jama," he said. "Now he's after you."

Sullivan suddenly looked over my shoulder, and whatever blood was left in his face drained away.

Before I could turn to look behind me, there was a sound like a lightning bolt and a huge comet of fiery pain crashed into my back. I screamed in agony and whirled around.

There stood Sirela, diamond-encrusted staff in hand, with a look of pure fury on her face.

48

THE SCOURGE

SAMIRA

I DIDN'T KNOW whose club this was, but between me, Aikan, Alla, Vane, the werewolf whores, crazy Malcolm, and his dumb dog Rosie, it was getting royally eff'd up. I stepped back from the ruckus and took a minute to relish the chaos—until some random vampire tried his luck with me.

I dodged a fist and returned one of my own. And that was all she wrote before he was cradling a broken jaw and hightailing it. I smirked as I watched him stumble his way out of the ruckus as fast as his wobbly-hobbly legs would carry him. Guess he wasn't about that life after all.

Aikan pulled up to me, and at the same time, our sharp eyes were seeing the same thing: the table, and its empty settings. Someone, or a group of someones, was supposed to have been here, and apparently, they hadn't shown up.

I stepped out of the way as one of the Lycana whorewolves threw a Magnate Club member over the bar. He toppled over it, spilling glasses and drinks. I followed him and finally saw and heard the faint *buzz* of a low-voltage electromagnetic field.

"A trap door," Aikan said.

He arrived behind the bar as I crashed my fist through the hidden control panel. After a dying spark, a door slid open in the mahogany paneling. Aikan and I shared a smile, and he walked through first. I followed, but before I disappeared, I shot a look at Alathia, busy yoking up Sullivan, tying up loose ends. Verifying that she was safe, I walked through.

The trek through the secret halls was short and quiet. Gun up and aimed, Aikan cleared the hallway quickly, all the while shielding me with his body. Maybe it was just me, but he seemed ex-military. That would explain a lot.

Still, I smiled; in all my life as a runt, I'd never had anyone watch out for me like this. Except for Alla. But never some tall, dark stranger, not like *this*. Hell, if this is what it was like to be a damsel in distress, then chile, sign me the hell up.

Aikan stopped, listening. But as a pureblood Lycana, I heard clear as day what he could only detect.

"This entire deal's gone completely tits up," someone hissed. "Security's down, and the dining room's a madhouse."

Three men, murmured amongst themselves. The conversation came from around the corner and farther down the hall. Only about 50 feet away from us. They continued.

"But what about Crimson Corp?"

"Sullivan's been made, and the Sirela-hag's exposed herself. Crimson's no longer a viable ally. The Scourge must move on to other opportunities."

Somehow the final voice seemed familiar. I closed my eyes, and my senses filled the space once more. Beams, wood, marble, and bodies all became lines and grids as a three-dimensional image developed in my mind.

"The Scourge ..." I whispered. "That enemy group you were talking about. They're here."

They stood in a tight circle, and by their body language, there was a lot of stress in the room.

Aikan took off, and I almost screamed at him to wait until I remembered that we were trying for the element of surprise. I clenched my fists and cursed his impulsiveness, finally feeling Alla's pain. If that man wasn't a werewolf, I was a mother duck.

I chased after him, and together, we burst into the secret room, ready to kick ass.

Somehow, though, not a single member of the Scourge looked surprised. Mainly because they were wearing masks. Mocking masks, artistic distortions of various Arcane creatures. Vampire, Nephilim, and werewolf.

Aikan snarled and tightened his grip on his gun. His eyes flickered in and out of their change as the wolf in him awoke. "I'm taking your heads with me tonight, you sons-of-bitches."

"Nice to see you again, Salek," the wolf-masked Scourge said. "And I see you've brought appealing company. How generous of you. When I last tortured you, I thought I'd made a bad impression. Clearly I was wrong."

The other two Scourge laughed, and my vision sharpened as I homed in on the speaker. I still couldn't see his face, but man, could I smell him. He smelled like blood. Benjamin Jamas's blood. Samantha Jamas's blood. And *werewolf* blood.

My hackles rose, and a feral growl escaped my throat. This caught his attention, and he tilted his head toward me.

But there was something else: the shadows moving along the wall. Black shapes rose from the floors, forming man-shaped figures. More Scourge members ... who were also Arcane. Arcane that I somehow couldn't hear, couldn't smell.

I took a step back, counting seven more Scourge assassins as they grew from shadow. Aikan took aim at the black masses.

"Fun fact, Samira Shaw," the Jama assassin, still looking at me, said. "Samantha Jama died slowly. And painfully. In the end, she begged for her life ... and I enjoyed listening."

That set something off in me *and* Aikan, and at the same time, we dove. The Scourge launched themselves at us, and the room exploded with violence, and blood, and magic.

49

FLESH-AND-BONE VICE

ALATHIA

"You," Sirela snarled. "Vampire!"

Her long titanium hair was swept up into a beehive and decorated with gemstone pins and a tiara. Her navy-blue velvet robe swept around her as if it had a life of its own, and her stilettos shimmering gold. She held her staff out toward me, and I aimed my revolver at her, ready for battle.

You, I wanted to reply. *Old, diamond-encrusted bitch.* My back was on fire, literally. I had to shrug my coat off. It lay burning on the floor, like autumn leaves. It was a shame. I liked that coat.

"You betrayed the Dominion," I said, brushing off residual flames from my shoulders, my gun still aimed squarely at the queen of the Conclave. Sullivan, still pinned to the luxurious wallpaper, trembled behind me. The rest of the room was a kangaroo circus.

"What do *you* know of the Dominion?" Sirela spat.

"I know that you're supposed to be protecting the Arcanes, but instead you decided to kill them."

Sirela's perfectly shaped eyebrows shot up. "Kill them? Is that what you think?"

"I know about EverDark. I know that you plan to imprison every were-wolf inside their human form."

She pursed her lips in a condescending way. "It's for the best, dear."

"It's social engineering," I said. "I won't accept that. And neither will the wolves."

"You've forgotten your history!"

I clenched my jaw. Of course, she would make it personal.

"Wolves have killed vampires for centuries," she said. "You know that."

Yes, I knew that. But just because a werewolf killed my father and destroyed my family didn't mean the entire breed should be wiped out.

Sirela stepped forward. "You lost everything."

"Not everything," I said.

Vane moved to join me and together we launched an attack. He sent a dart of magic her way and I fired my gun. Sirela dodged the magic that sheared through the air, but the silver bullet caught her in the shoulder. She yelled and dropped her staff, falling back, but recovered and stayed on her feet. She straightened up, hand on her wounded shoulder, and glared at me. Shock waves reverberated in the room. No one shoots the head of the Cloud Conclave.

Sirela's face contorted with pain. "We did it to maintain the peace."

"Wrong," I said. "You did it to make your job easier. To free up time to better plunder the resources of the realm."

"It was to be a peaceful revolution until you stuck your nose in," she said.

"I didn't stick anything in. I was brought in. You know that, because you're the one who ordered it."

"Brought in so we could keep an eye on you," Sirela said. "I know what a troublemaker you are. But you've gone too far in coming here. You know too much."

"Step down, Sirela," said Vane. "It's not too late."

Her eyes flickered to Vane. "Traitor!" she roared. She moved her hand from her shoulder—which she had managed to heal—and stretched it out toward Vane and me. Her staff lay on the floor, but that didn't stop her from sending another bolt of magic my way. Before I could stop it or step aside, a meteor of fire and sparks smashed into me, and I was knocked to the ground. Another bolt incinerated Vane's wand in his hand. I couldn't see properly through the smoke, I saw that half of his hand was taken along with the blast. He shouted in shock and agony and fell to the floor beside me, grasping his burning fingers.

Fury was like a white light inside of me. It burst through me, razing my pain, fear, and confusion. I was so angry I could have walked on burning coals. I stood up and hissed, ready to take Sirela's head off. She reached for her staff, but I beat her to it. Instead, she grasped my neck. I was once again on the floor, writhing under her grip. Her strength was immense—how much was a spell and how much was real? Her grip got tighter and tighter, a magical flesh-and-bone vice around my neck.

She crushed my windpipe and kept pushing. My lungs became sirens, desperate for air. My body faded to numb. I tried to fight back but Sirela transformed into a monster in my mind: all-powerful, all-consuming. A hissing medusa, a glowing Shiva, a hungry kraken devouring a sinking ship. I dropped my gun and the staff. My vision dimmed, except for golden stars that sparked before me. The strength left my limbs and I had nothing left. Just smoke, stars, and shattered dreams.

50

CASSIAN

SAMIRA

THUNDER ROARED through the room as Aikan emptied his clip, his spectacular aim and magically charged bullets striking down four of the Scourge. I tore through three more of them, and as he took on the remaining two, I turned my glare to the wolf-masked Jama assassin.

For a second, he stared at me. Then he ran! WTF. All that big talk ...

I lunged after him, crossing the room in a couple of leaps and ramming my way through the door. He was just up ahead. I flew down the hallway after him. He was fast, faster than any normal human, and did I just see a tail—?

He turned and fired, and I dodged, feeling the silver's acidic heat burn the air around me as the bullets missed me. His aim was trash this time, and my senses were sharper than ever. He couldn't shake me. His gun ran dry, and he discarded it just as he slammed through the door at the end of the hall. As the door swung closed, I went quadruped and pounced.

He turned and raised his hands as I landed on him, and we tumbled into the night. Our bodies rolled over each other through the Magnate Club gardens, and as we tussled, I tore off his disguise.

"You feral little BITCH!!"

He slammed his knuckles into my temple and threw me off him. I landed in a roll and somehow got to my paws. But what I saw when he stood up in the light haunted me.

"Holy gonzola cheese ..." Tears filled my eyes. "Cassian?"

The man standing there just smirked at me. He was tall like me. Dark like me. Strong like me. But unlike me, he hadn't been abandoned. His name, along with five others, was the only thing I'd taken with me when I was exiled.

Cassian: assassin of the Scourge. And my big brother.

For a moment, only the wind spoke between us. I was a statue. A million questions filled my mind, but they were nothing compared to the agony that now spread through my chest. Was this it? Was *this* the information Aikan had been holding back the entire time?

"Cass ..." I couldn't manage much else.

Cassian looked off and sneered. "Little sister. Fancy meeting you here."

"You tried to kill me," I snarled. "At Jama's house. Why?"

"Didn't know it was you at first. But if you're looking for an apology, I'm afraid that's not going to happen. You weren't supposed to live anyway, so..."

"Where the hell have you been? And why are you working with the Scourge? They're trying to kill us! They're trying to wipe out all werewolves!"

He shrugged. "Let's just say that a life of running on all fours and sniffing asses wasn't for me."

My inner wolf snarled at that. Sounded like the same kind of prejudiced insults that vamps and other Arcanes threw at werewolves. Whenever they could get away with it, that was. Cassian had been completely brainwashed. And what was worse, he didn't even care.

"So because you're a self-hating creep, you decided to join the same psychos who want to wipe all werewolves out? Have you lost your mind?"

"The Scourge and Crimson Corp might not always be on the same page as far as Arcanes go. But on one thing we agree—the werewolves have to go. They are a danger to the human population and need to be eliminated."

I was shaking my head, refusing to hear him. "No ... No, Cass. You've lost it."

"No, dear sister. On the contrary, I've found it. The Scourge is doing God's work. We keep the planet in the hands of those to whom it *belongs*. The human race."

"Except you'll *never* be human, Cass. Ever."

"Oh, but Damon Sullivan is very much on the verge of changing that. For good. Through *this*."

He removed his hand from his jacket pocket, and in the moonlight, he held up a capsule of EverDark. Immediately, I remembered that I had four fresh doses pumping through my veins.

"No worries, little sister. It would take *way* more dosing with this baby to kill the werewolf in you. Especially a purebred one. Trust me, you'll be able to go back to biting fleas off your ass in a few hours."

I bit down and tightened my fists.

"Me, on the other hand?" He continued. "I'm nearly there. And between this and the Scourge, we'll be able to get rid of the werewolves for good."

"You must make Mother so proud."

"When I see her again, I'll ask her." He smiled. "She was our first test subject."

That ripped a hole in me, and the werewolf jumped right through it. Right at *him*. I attacked, shifting into full werewolf form as I pounced.

We fell deeper into the garden, and I went full-on feral: biting, clawing, ripping at him and his clothes. In the flurry of fur and claws, he snarled, somehow got his feet under my ribcage, and pushed me off with surprising strength. I flew back and landed, but in the next second, I was on my four feet again.

Under the moonlight, Cassian began to bend, to *change*. His limbs cracked and his skin stretched, and as he spasmed, the man who once stood on two feet now crouched on four. My eyes widened, taking in the information faster than my brain could process it.

He was going werewolf, EverDark be damned.

He was finally done, and he turned to me. My body froze as two blood-red and yellow eyes cut the night. The black pupils within them contracted as he took me in. This thing before me was not quite werewolf ... he was a horrible deformed hybrid of werewolf and EverDark demon. The same creature that had chased me through the halls of Crimson Corp.

"Come, little sister." The demonic voice of what used to be my brother shook the trees, collapsed the air in the night. "Come die."

My hackles rose, and my lips peeled back from my fangs. I snarled, and at the same time, I thought of our mom, of how she might be suffering.

Give me your power.

My lupine prayer went to the moon, and somehow, the goddess

responded, filling me, lending me her strength. I felt myself grow, felt the soil sink under my massive paws, heard nature bow before me.

"Not until you die first," I growled.

He leaped and at the same time, so did I. Our bodies met and clashed, two storm fronts of immortal fury tearing up the night. I threw everything I had at the monster, and finally, one of us found an opening, reared back, and chomped down on the other's neck.

Hard.

Blood sprayed, painting the grass with a Pollock of crimson, and a howl tore through the night, laced with the rattle of death.

51

DEEP, DARK, DEAD

ALATHIA

My vision faded into nothing, and my consciousness sprinted after it, into the dark. Everything leaked away, including the pain of Sirela's hands around my neck and my exploding heart. Sounds got more and more muffled until there was just silence, as if I were lying at the bottom of the ocean. Deep, dark, dead. There, I thought to myself. My tired heart had eventually stopped beating.

But then a noise cut through the dim silence, a dagger in the darkness, slicing it open. My eyes flew open, my swollen face near bursting from the pressure of Sirela's grip. I tried to move one last time, tried to fight for my life, but my limbs were still deep beneath the heavy water. I heard that sound again. I couldn't place it until I saw a blurry Rosie sailing through the air. She had leaped off the royal table and landed on Sirela, who uttered a shocked scream and let go of me. Rosie didn't waste any time in chomping down on Sirela's neck.

I had never loved a dog as much as I loved that little pug right then.

Malcolm rushed over, bruised, bleeding, clothes torn, and wrenched Rosie away from the evil woman before the pup could get hurt. It gave me just enough time to reach for Sirela's staff. Without hesitating, I smashed the diamond knob as hard as I could against her jeweled head. It made a nightmarish noise. I think the whole room heard her skull crack. She fell sideways and landed on the floor, eyes like marbles.

I cursed in Croatian. Had I just killed the most powerful woman in the Dominion?

Vane crawled up to me, injured hand tucked against his midriff. He placed his other hand gently on my head.

"Are you okay?" he asked urgently. "Are you okay?"

My larynx crushed, I whispered back to him in a voice that sounded like sandpaper. "Is she dead?"

He frowned and looked over at Sirela's still body, then went over to her and felt for a pulse.

"Alive," he said, and took the invisible handcuffs from his robe and chained her wrists together.

Malcolm helped me up; unsteady on my feet but able to stand. Sullivan's cries reached me. He was still nailed to the wall with the golden cutlery, and the wolves were sniffing him over.

"Let me go," he said, "Please."

I was tempted to leave him to the wolves. Instead, I walked over to him, slipped my hand into his expensive blazer pocket, and pulled out his phone.

"You know what to do," I said.

52

OMEGA FREE

SAMIRA

LYING IN THE GRASS, I breathed heavily, blood seeping into the ground under me ... from Cassian's neck.

He lay beside me, breathing hard and unable to move. I'd gotten him in the jugular. He was at least three times bigger than I was, but I was and faster, with easier access to his vulnerable bits.

Guess there *were* some advantages to being a runt.

"You ..." he struggled to breathe. "Earned ... a stripe."

Across my shoulder, a stripe burned brightly in the night. The mark of defeating an alpha. I'd finally earned my first.

"So what?" I muttered. I didn't look at him. "Is it going to bring back the mother you killed?"

"You idiot ... Mom's not ... dead ..."

I sat up, looking at him. "Then where is she, Cas?"

"Don't know ... she escaped our facility years ago."

His eyes rolled back. He was fading fast. As I looked at him, I gritted my teeth, struggling with my choices. I tore into my own paw with my fangs, exposing a ragged patch of flesh and releasing blood. Then I put my paw in his mouth, giving him the blood.

The drops slid down his throat. Simultaneously, his body changed, shedding the shell of the EverDark demon. Slowly, his brown fur grew through; thin, but a good sign. His body was accepting the transfusion.

I watched the wide wound on his neck heal. He reverted to his human form again, and in the next moment, he struggled to his feet. I got there first, though, still in werewolf form.

"Try me, Cass," I snarled. "Try me again, and this time, I'll tear your head clean off."

But he was drained, exhausted. Defeated and knocked to the bottom of his pack, which was clearly the Scourge. They weren't exactly a werewolf pack, but as a team of assassins, I assumed they wouldn't take his failure lightly. His face showed signs of unease. Fear.

"I'm going to find Mom," I said. "And our brothers and sisters. I will also smoke out your asshole friends in the Scourge and wipe them off the planet."

He looked at me with contempt.

"I'll let you live," I said. "And you can spend the rest of your life in the Cloud Conclave's prison. If you try to escape, if you try in any way to contact the Scourge, or if you ever try to hurt anyone I care about ever again, I will rip you to shreds."

He sneered as he fell against a nearby tree. "Whatever, kid."

A blink and then I was behind him, pushing his naked body forward with a snarl, toward the rest of my team. He grunted but reluctantly obeyed. Hands high in the air, he shuffled forward.

My heart swelled. I was the baddest bitch of the season. I knew it. Because Samira Shaw, the abandoned, hot-headed, omega-level runt, had just kicked an EverDark demon's ass, arrested a member of the Scourge, and got a lead on her family.

And she lived to tell the tale.

By the time we returned to the club gardens, I was back in human form and fully dressed. The Cloud Conclave enforcers took Cassian into custody, but not before he spat blood at my feet. I sneered and turned my back on him for the last time.

"SAMI!"

Alla ran up to me, poring over my wounds, and rattling off questions. With all her nitpicking, I must've looked really bad. She looked frazzled herself, so by rights, she had no business being all "motherly" with me.

"How was Sirela?" I smirked.

"A bitch and a half," she muttered, indicating her own wounds. "But I don't think she'll be ruling over much anymore, considering she just tried to wipe out all werewolves. She's in the Conclave's custody."

"Good. Hopefully she hobbled away with her wrists in cuffs and that diamond staff halfway up her ass."

Alla looked at me, and the pinch of sadness in her eyes made evident what she wanted to ask.

"I'm fine," I said quietly. "A little shaken up, but ... fine."

Before she said anything more, I stepped forward to find Aikan.

He stood in the moonlight, smack in the middle of the garden, staring up at the sky. He looked totally trashed; cuts, burns, and bruises narrated his own fight in the bowels of the Magnate Club. As he gazed at the moon, his injuries began to heal.

Huh. More wolf than human after all.

Everyone else was not quite so lucky. Still alive, though, thankfully.

Malcolm was a hot mess, and Rosie sat proudly behind him. Looked as though she kicked some ass tonight and also ate a lot of chicken, and that made me proud. Manic Malcolm scribbled copious notes and took bright flashy pictures—until Aikan yanked his camera out of his hand, broke it, and snarled at him.

Meanwhile, the werewolf girls had shifted back to human form and moon-tanned naked on the grass. Normally, they'd all be in werewolf form, but the EverDark seemed to have that under control tonight.

Alpha bitch Alinka was fully dressed and didn't have a scratch on her; guess she was too pretty to throw 'bows. She handed out spare clothes to her pack and delivered a cold lecture about their "pack form."

As I approached, one of the werechicks jumped up, brushed past Alinka, and ran up to me. Surprisingly, the other werewolves followed.

"Wow, Samira! You kicked that guy's ass!" she gushed.

"Yeah, we all saw it! It was totally boss!" another piped up.

"And that jumping, twisting, morphing-in-the-air thing!"

"YEAH!" they all said together.

My face burned up. "Oh! Well ... thank you?" I had no idea that anyone might have seen the fight, but we did have supervision. They probably watched from right here, pay-per-view style.

"Show us how to do it!"

"Yeah, please?"

"That was ... very brave of you, Samira."

The voice belonged to Lila, Jama's mistress. Dried blood was smattered across her face, but from the smell of it, it wasn't hers.

"Not really," I snickered. "I think I may just have anger issues."

"I meant choosing what's right over joining your brother's cause," she continued. "That was very brave."

I lowered my eyes. "It was an easy choice, not a brave one. I mean, join my family in the destruction of all werewolves, or not. Pretty much a no-brainer."

"Not for most wolves. Not for those who've always had a family."

"I never have." And then it hit me, crushed me. "And ... I guess I never will."

Lila smiled gently and put a hand on my shoulder. "Well, how would you like to join ours?"

"That's *enough*, Lila."

I turned to see Alinka standing behind them. Fuming. "You've given the omega runt her compliments," she continued. "And that's far more than she's earned."

Alinka closed the distance, her eyes more threatening than ever. The crowd parted around her as she got in my face. She sneered and flicked my nose. To put me in my place. My fists clenched, but still, I didn't swing.

"If you want to join our pack, you can be our jester," she snickered. "Can you dance, *runt?*"

I finally looked in her eyes. Hard. "Only if I get to do a two-step on your face, bitch."

She growled and stepped forward. I didn't budge, but I lifted the torn patch of jacket from my shoulder, showing her the stripe I'd just earned.

"I just ripped the shit out of my own brother who's three times my size, and I sent him to prison with his tail between his legs. I might be an omega, but I can literally mow this entire lawn with your ass, so do *not* fuck with me!"

Alinka's eyes widened. The entire pack drew in a collective breath, but I kept going. Because I was officially tired of her grade-A bullshit.

"I have no interest in joining your pack, or your family. Because you know what? I already *have* a family," I snapped. I looked at Alla, who smiled back warmly. "So you can take your offer and shove it up your Brazilian-waxed asshole. Have a good goddamned evening."

Crickets chirped in the night, filling in the silence that Alinka couldn't fill herself. I didn't wait for a response. I turned and walked away. As I did, I felt her wide surprised eyes on my back, and suddenly I heard the snickers of her pack assault her. I was still alone. But whatever. Because that also meant I was finally free.

Omega free.

EPILOGUE: DE OPPRESSO LIBER

ALATHIA

THE DAY WAS SUNNY. Usually, I'm not a huge fan of that fiery star, but today it seemed right. We had rooted out the dark heart of the Masquerade and set it ablaze. We had toppled the evil queen who had been leaking poison into our realm.

DE OPPRESSO LIBER

The oppressed will be liberated

We had also avenged the murder of Veronica Jama's father. I squeezed her small hand. It was cold, and a sharp contrast to the warm weather. She knew the whole story now. Maybe she was too young to hear it, but she deserved to know. Her new guardian—a friendly-looking aunt from her mother's side—had given us some time to talk in the front garden, but now it was time for me to go.

On my way out, Veronica stopped me, her solemn eyes searching mine.

"Will you be back?" she asked.

I remembered how abandoned I had felt as an orphan; how I had reached out seeking anyone who would have me and came back empty-handed.

I lowered myself, knee on the grass, to be on her level. "Would you like me to come back?"

She nodded.

"All right," I said, and almost immediately regretted it. What on earth would I do with a child? I could bring a toy. I could take her for a milkshake. Would a guardian allow a vampire to take a little girl out for a milkshake?

The woman gave me a tight smile and put a protective hand on her niece's shoulder. Veronica gave me a slow wave, and I returned it. As I walked away, a thought occurred to me, and I turned back to her.

"You were right, you know."

They both frowned at me, not knowing what I was referring to.

"The Bad Man," I said. "It was a woman."

Edgar was waiting for me outside, the sleek Jaguar purring in welcome. I climbed into the air-conditioned interior with a feeling of relief. Vane put away his phone and smiled at me.

"How did that go?" he asked. "Ready for a stiff drink?"

"It's ten in the morning," I said, although I appreciated his enthusiasm. In bed, in talking, in drinking the Croatian vodka I like. I felt like his keen spirit warmed my cold one.

"I was just checking the stock market," he said. "Crimson Corp's stock has crashed. The market analysts are describing it as blood on the streets."

"Ha," I said.

"But their competitor—what are they called again?"

"Red Kite," I said.

"Red Kite shares have shot through the roof. Apparently they had a very generous cash injection from an anonymous donor, which is allowing them to take up the reins as the country's major synth-blood supplier."

"That's good news," I said.

"You didn't happen to have anything to do with that, did you?"

Edgar accelerated. I looked out of the window, watching the trees and buildings haze into each other, and smiled to myself.

I would have liked to have left Damon Sullivan to the wolves, but something had come over me, some kind of mercy that I was not used to feeling. Instead, I struck a deal. I'd let him go, let him flee to another country to live a better life; be a better man. And he would pay us for the job he had hired us for. I had allowed him one call that night at the trashed Magnate Club ... to his private banker.

Sullivan's payment had been very generous. Not only had he paid us what he owed, but he had—at my suggestion—added a hefty tip. The lump sum had been enough to pay Samira her half, bail out her charity case, and send some seed capital over to Red Kite. They would have to fire on all cylinders to meet the vampires' need for synth now that Crimson was nothing more than a bloodstained memory.

There had been thousands left over for the smaller things. A stipend for Malcolm (although he turned it down), a generous raise for Edgar, a new wand for Vane, and a total overhaul of my home and office security system.

"Miss Laurent," said Edgar. He was wearing a rather dashing new suit. "My grandson was absolutely thrilled with that Star Wars LEGO set you sent him for his birthday." His eyes twinkled in the rearview mirror, and Vane absentmindedly put his bandaged hand on my knee. It was healing, but it would never be the same.

"He was completely over the moon," said Edgar.

Over the moon.

EverDark.

It gave me flashbacks of the battle. The damage done, magic spilled, and lives lost. And it made me think of Samira. She had disappeared to New York again. This time I wasn't sure if she'd come back. It hurt, but that was battery love.

I put my hand gently over Vane's as the trees rushed outside the window. I turned to the wizard, looked into his eyes, a ceaseless and steady beat in my chest. He gazed at me tenderly and clicked his fingers, creating a golden spark between us. Sometimes he did that; little tricks just for my amusement. A smile twitched at my lips, and I couldn't help feeling a small flame of hope for the future. My deathless heart was alive. My dead finch had awoken.

∼

SHAW & SALEK, INC

SAMIRA

I was back in New York City and already rushing back into the Happy Days office, looking a mess.

"I'm here! I'm here, I'm here! SO sorry I took so long!" I shouted.

I didn't complain about the fact that no one responded. Because like I said, I looked a *mess*. I'd had just enough time to hop to the bathroom and get myself together ... *and* to whisk on that new musky eyeshadow I'd swiped from Alla just that morning.

I stumbled into the bathroom and peered into the mirror. Oh *GOD*.

One of my afro puffs was perfect; the other, a mess. My jacket was inside out, and my shoes were on the wrong feet. Cray-cray.

"Don't worry, Sami. You look beautiful. You always do."

I whirled around, brandishing my afro pick and my lip gloss. I pointed them at the stalls behind me like weapons of war, when out stepped Aikan, from the one by the door.

Again. And I hadn't heard or detected him. *Again*.

"WHAT IS UP WITH YOU BEING CREEPY IN BATH-ROOMS?" I shrieked. "And did you *really* lure me here with that fake phone call?"

He laughed. "No. They really *were* short on staff, and they called me too. Believe it or not, I *do* volunteer here."

"Since when?"

He smirked, and his eyes flickered. "Since now."

I made a face and shoved my stuff back into my pocketbook. I crossed my arms.

"Oh, come now, Sami. I was waiting in the foyer, but when I heard you get off the elevator, I couldn't help myself." He flashed me a winning smile and opened the door wide behind him. "Take a walk with me?"

I narrowed my eyes suspiciously. "*Where?*"

His eyes twinkled.

Central Park was gorgeous today, a perfect spring blush of flora and fauna, and Aikan had taken full advantage. When we reached the clearing, I gasped: he'd laid out a spread under a beautiful willow tree by the lake. A complete picnic, French-style. We kicked off our shoes and settled for a long, needed lunch.

"This is amazing," I muttered. The high blush on my cheeks hid behind my skin, but it was there. "Thank you, Aikan. You're very sweet."

"With as much ass you kicked the past three days? You deserve it. And, well ... you *did* ask me on that date."

"WHAT?!"

"Nothing."

We shared a gaze, and for the first time, I felt electricity zap through me. The man was gorgeous, and I guess it took bullets not flying my way for me to truly appreciate it. My skin burned, and I looked away, bashful.

Aikan stuffed a sandwich into his mouth and stretched over the blanket, enjoying the sun. "You know, we can actually afford to do this more often now that we're paid. If nothing else, Crimson Corp's checks don't bounce."

I raised an eyebrow. "Crimson Corp paid *you* too? How'd that happen."

He smiled secretly. "Well! With all my pain and suffering I endured at

Crimson, let's just say Sullivan was willing to settle out of court. To the tune of, oh … millions?"

My eyes widened. "Wow. You're quite the businessman."

"I do okay. And now, you do too."

"Wait … what?"

"I noticed that somehow Happy Days' Orphanage is mysteriously out of debt—"

"Wait, how did you know that?"

"—but virtually none of your payment from Crimson went to your expenses."

"And how did you know *that*?!"

"I told you, my people can hack into wherever they need to be."

"Why do 'your people' need to be all up in my business?" I snapped.

"You're a newly discovered werewolf. We keep track of all our own, take care of our own. Runt or not. And now, we're taking care of you. *I* am taking care of you."

A high color spread over my face. "Aikan, I don't think—"

"Your bills are paid," his words bulldozed over mine. "All of them, including your debts and your rent for the next year. So now, you can breathe easy."

My breath caught in my throat, choking me. "I—don't know what to— thank you." I looked away, my skin on fire. A long silence between us. Then: "Aikan, don't take this the wrong way. I love all this and really, really appreciate it."

"But?"

"But. Why? And don't tell me that 'your team' sent you. Why are you doing this? Why are you here? You know, now that Crimson Corp is trashed and all?"

"You rejected two packs," he stated.

"I—*yes*? But what does that have to do with you?"

"Well." He shifted, and for the first time, he seemed sheepish. "I don't have one either. So ... maybe we should form our own?"

I raised an eyebrow. Shoved half a sandwich into my mouth. "But, I'm already on a team with Alathia. It's not a *pack*, but—"

"Yeah, but she's in *Jo'burg*. Recently, there have been more and more sightings of Arcanes in NYC too. You've heard of the HOHEA team, the Godsman ... yeah?"

I nod. I *had* heard of them. All total badasses, but also as elusive as the information surrounding them. The Hitmen of Happily Ever After (HOHEA) were on an entirely different level of Arcane; in fact, they didn't even call themselves that, as they dealt only with the most dangerous and sinister magickals, like mob bosses and other high profile targets. And the Godsman, well, the name pretty much spoke for itself.

"While they're all busy handling the elite," Aikan continued, "—eventually someone will need to keep the peace on the ground. Might as well be us."

"I ... I don't know ..."

My words were unsure, but in truth, his ideas sounded downright delicious. Forming our own pack? Fighting magickal bad guys in NYC? More French picnics and Happy Days' barbecues, for free? Baller.

But it wouldn't be just fun and games. Alla and I had already made quite a name for ourselves by keeping the Arcane and human worlds separate and safe. And between Alla's recent takedown of Sirela and my arrest of a Scourge assassin, well, business was pretty sweet. With that kind of reputation, creating a satellite site with our new allies and spreading positive influence only made sense.

"The Scourge is still out there," Aikan pushed on, piling on reasons. "So are the rest of your siblings, and somewhere, your mom. And so is the cure for what Crimson Corp and the Scourge did to me. Both personally and professionally, our interests are mutual, Sami. And unless Alla focuses all her efforts and money on finding your family *and* ending the Scourge, you'll need some help."

He was right. Alla wasn't heartless. Of course, she'd want to help bring the Scourge down. And she probably would, in some way. But she also wasn't Braveheart, nor was she Captain America of the Avengers. Look up "ultimate anti-heroine" in the dictionary, and you'd find Alla's picture right there, resting bitch face and all. She liked keeping the balance. That was pretty much it.

What Aikan was suggesting, though, was a different thing entirely. *He* wanted to take down an enemy empire. And he wanted my help.

When I finally turned back to him, I was beaming, the yes smattered all over my face. "I'm in. But *only* part-time. I won't leave Alla hanging in Jo'burg cold turkey."

He grinned like a kid on Christmas. "Fantastic. Part-time it is. What should we call ourselves?"

Him uttering the word "us" made my heart flutter, but I tried to ignore it so I could think. Finally, a smirk spread itself across my face, and when our gazes matched, I knew he was thinking the same thing. "Let's call it ... Shaw & Salek, Inc."

THE END

Thanks for reading!

If you'd like to check out more books by JT Lawrence, including a new kick-ass vampire-slaying female wizard detective 6-book series, visit her website at

www.jt-lawrence.com

"This is a sizzling hot book. The characters are great, the plot races and the writing is great. Humour, magic, crossbows, ferrets, mysterious men – this book has it all. I can't wait for the rest of the books in this series."
– Amazon reviewer

ABOUT JT LAWRENCE

JT Lawrence is a USA Today bestselling author and playwright. She lives in Parkview, Johannesburg, in a house with a red front door.

Be notified of giveaways & new releases by signing up to JT's mailing list at

www.jt-lawrence.com

facebook.com/JanitaTLawrence

twitter.com/pulpbooks

instagram.com/authorjtlawrence

amazon.com/author/jtlawrence

bookbub.com/profile/jt-lawrence

4. The Ember Isles

5. The Chaos Jar

6. The New Dawn Throne

STANDALONE NOVELS

The Memory of Water

Grey Magic

SHORT STORY COLLECTIONS

Sticky Fingers

Sticky Fingers 2

Sticky Fingers 3

Sticky Fingers 4

Sticky Fingers 5

Sticky Fingers 6

Sticky Fingers: 36 Deliciously Twisted Short Stories: The Complete Box Set
Collection (Books 1 - 3)

NON-FICTION

The Underachieving Ovary

ABOUT COLBY R. RICE

SCI-FI & FANTASY NOVELIST.
SCREENWRITER.
HORROR, ACTION, AND SCI-FI FILM DIRECTOR.
GAME WRITER & NARRATIVE DESIGNER.
GLOBETROTTER & POLYGLOT.
FABLE HUNTER. ACTION JUNKIE. REBEL RAGDOLL.

A shameless nerd and bookworm since the age of five, Colby R. Rice is the author of The Given and The Taken, the first two novels in The Books of Ezekiel, a dystopian sci-fi and urban fantasy mega-novel decalogy.

She was an Air Force BRAT born in Bitburg Rheinland-Pfalz,

Germany and came to the States at the age of one. Colby bounced around a lot but finally settled in Tucson, where she could at last deal with her addictions to writing, legends & mythology, filmmaking, creative entrepreneurship, motorcycles, and traveling.

Now, armed with a mound of animal crackers and gallons of Coca-Cola, Colby takes on the fiction writing trinity (novel writing, screenwriting, and game writing) in a fight to the death!

A former (recovering) PhD student and research methodologist, she is now somehow an MFA student in the Generative Dramaturgy program at the University of Arizona, where she is studying for her third degree, diving into her eighth language (Russian), and doing cool theatre stuff (like directing, dramaturgy, and playwriting)!

Current creative projects include: the next slew of novels in *The Books of Ezekiel* series, the first two novels in a New Adult dystopian series, the first novel in an urban fantasy crime noir(e) series, the development of her first horror feature film, and the growth of her media f'empire-in-progress, Rebel Ragdoll, LLC. Stay tuned to her website http://colbyrrice.com (or her social media nests below) for updates on her creative projects!

facebook.com/ColbyRRicePage

twitter.com/ColbyRRice

instagram.com/ColbyRRice

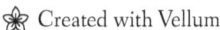 Created with Vellum

www.ingramcontent.com/pod-product-compliance
Lightning Source LLC
Chambersburg PA
CBHW052033240626
47153CB00006B/2062